P9-CJN-052

GIRLS,
VISIONS
AND
EVERY
THING

SARAH
SCHULMAN

The Seal Press

Copyright ©1986 by Sarah Schulman.

All rights reserved. No part of this book may be reproduced in any form, except for brief reviews, without the written permission of the publisher.

Girls, Visions and Everything was published with the help of the National Endowment for the Arts.

Published by The Seal Press, 500 East Pike, Seattle, Washington 98122.

Library of Congress Cataloging-in-Publication Data

Schulman, Sarah 1958-
  Girls, visons, and everything.

  I. Title.
PS3569.C5393G5   1986   813'.54   86-17692
ISBN   0-931188-38-5 (pbk.)

Cover design by Deborah Brown.
Text design by Laurie Becharas and Faith Conlon.
Composition by Scarlet Letters, Seattle.

Printed in the United States of America.

First edition, September 1986.
10 9 8 7 6 5 4 3 2 1

ACKNOWLEDGMENTS

I am very grateful to everyone who took the time to read this manuscript and to discuss it with me in detail, especially Beryl Satter, Julie Scher, Stephanie Doba and Teal Frasier. I am also thankful to Maxine Wolfe and Bettina Berch for their attention and recommendations, and to Peg Byron and Leslie Gervirtz for the champagne.

I also want to thank Sally Brunsman, Faith Conlon and Barbara Wilson for their intelligent and precise editorial work.

This is a work of fiction. The author in no way means to suggest that any of the events described in this text actually happened. Furthermore, none of the actions or words of any of the characters are meant to be accurate representations of any words or actions of real persons living or dead. The personalities and events described in this work are the products of the author's imagination.

For Susan Young

Girls, Visions and Everything

PART ONE

ONE

Lila Futuransky always knew she was an outlaw, but she could never figure out which one. She wanted to be free but couldn't decide what that meant. Yet, endlessly persevering, she continued to believe that she could construct any kind of life that she desired to live. And, because she both understood the phenomenon of process and felt that, at twenty-five, she was still young and had time, she continued to be a general dyke about town, alternately entertaining and antagonizing the people she bumped into, tripped over, walked with and the women that she slept with.

Lila felt pretty good about herself that night in May, on her way to meet Helen Hayes at ten. Her black hair stood up, all spikey and energized by a brand new haircut that was half queer, half punk. She had a Jack Kennedy jaw and a Katharine Hepburn dazzle and she wore her pants tight. Her tank top was silky and showed the shape of her breasts whenever she wanted them to be seen.

This date with Helen confirmed in Lila's mind that she had perfected that combination of softness and electricity that let her pick out the women she wanted to sleep with and then enabled her to do so. Waving to Ray, a friendly drug dealer working the corner of Saint Mark's and First, she walked into The Pyramid Club with complete confidence. This time, she was sure, everything would turn out right.

Despite Helen's reputation as female trouble, Lila had resolved to make love to her after three viewings of Helen's show *The Girls in Apartment Twelve A* at the local lesbian clubhouse known informally as The Kitsch-Inn. What had attracted her to Helen in the first place was her pop-television combination of neurosis and sick genius. As though lesbianism was just another category on *Hollywood Squares*. Helen's delivery was somewhere between Gloria Swanson and *Gilligan's Island*. There were always lines about being wet and breathless at the shopping mall. Plus, Helen was little and skinny and physically vulnerable and jerky-looking. Lila thought she was just so cute. Finally, after carefully planning her delivery to correspond to Helen's aesthetic sensibility, Lila walked right over to her and said,

"So Helen, when are we going to have an affair?"

"Anytime you want," Helen replied, batting her false eyelashes and wriggling up too close. "I've actually been considering you too, Lila, for a little cheap and meaningless sex."

Lila had guessed right on the button. Helen was not the sentimental type.

"But not too cheap," Lila said. She'd see what color Helen's nipples were, and how she liked to have them touched. They'd have fun together and feel good about each other later.

"I'm free tomorrow night," Helen said, "after the show at The Pyramid Club. I'll leave your name on the guest list."

And there it was, right on the guest list, just like Helen had said it would be. There was no reason to be nervous, the whole thing was sewn up. Now Lila could just sit back and enjoy it. The star of her own personal movie, Lila ordered a scotch and boldly put herself in the front row to look closely at Helen's little body and watch her deliver those lines with a perfected East Village deadpan. The audience was in-the-know enough to go for it and Helen had them right where she wanted them.

When the show was over, Lila casually held back, letting the crowd cluster around Helen with handshakes and kisses, who handled the attention with a skill derived from a precise combination of grace, diplomacy and fierce ambition. Lila figured she'd make her way over there when the place thinned out. Here's the scenario she had in her head:

"Great show, Helen."

"Now that you're here it's going to get even better."

"I liked watching you up there in that polyester dress."

"Oh Lila, you're so observant. So, why don't I change my clothes and then you can come home with me for a little brewsky and the other delights that await you. I've been thinking about that tongue of yours all day long."

Lila mulled over these lines, wondering if they were the right shade of camp to please Miss Hayes. She really wanted to please Miss Hayes. Where was Miss Hayes? Lila was searching by the video games when Helen whizzed by, surrounded by her entourage. Lila sinkingly followed.

"Helen," she hissed, "what's going on?"

"I'm in love," she said, over her shoulder.

"What?"

"I meant to call you, but we just had an all-afternoon honeymoon."

"You meant to call me?"

Helen looked up from under her pillbox hat.

"Just put it on hold Lila, there's still something there. Just put it on hold."

What an actress. She was so rude, it was practically art. So, now Lila had mud in her eye. She had serious mud in her eye.

TWO

W hen the dust cleared Lila was standing alone on the sidewalk almost giving in to tears. But, priding herself on her good nature and ability to rebound from any situation, she walked back, softly, into the Pyramid Club. Leaning on the bar for a moment to regain her composure, she glanced around the place, to make sure there were no witnesses. Then she saw Emily Harrison sitting quietly on a corner stool looking demure in a neato black lace hat of her own making.

"Hi Emily, I just got mud in my eye. You know what that means? I just got humiliated by a woman. Shit. Want to dance with me?"

It was Thelma Houston singing *Don't Leave Me This Way*. They boogied around a bit, sort of weirdly, until Lila tried to really dance, twirl her and everything. To her surprise, she ended up being twirled instead, since Emily's arms were much stronger than she anticipated. Still, they never did quite get in sync with each other.

"Hey Emily. You feel like talking? I kinda want to talk."

They walked outside, headed towards the Kitsch-Inn where Emily spent every spare moment working on shows. She'd been sleeping there too, on the make-up table, when nothing else was available. It was hot for May, everyone was out on the street. The sky was clear.

"So Lila, what do you want to talk about?" Emily's face was shining in the night light. Lila couldn't look her in the eye, and watched the city instead as they walked along on the sidewalk. Lila felt okay about Emily. She didn't know her very well. They'd only been together over a few joints. It was always a fun conversation which would end very politely as though nothing really important or intimate had gone on. Still, it had occurred to her that Emily had a chameleon's beauty. She was bland in a crowd but somehow mysteriously alluring one on one, if anybody bothered to look.

The first time Lila every noticed her was in a performance at The Kitsch-Inn. It was a lesbian version of *A Streetcar Named Desire* and Emily was Stella Kowalski. She'd looked exactly like Stella with thin arms in a sleeveless cotton dress, clearly defined neck bones, a few lines in her face. Like she really was pretty, but just a little tired.

"That Stanley," she'd said, and Lila had really believed she was Stella, picturing how her naked legs would wrap around Marlon Brando when he carried her off to make love.

"Stella's not strong," Emily said, sitting on the floor of the Inn, "but she has balance. I'm the same way. I work at a textile factory, always lifting things, working the machinery, and the guys can't figure out where the power comes from. They think it's cute. It turns them on."

Lila understood why. Emily was attractive in a soft way, the kind of pretty that deceived men into thinking they could easily have her because that's what that kind of pretty women are for.

"Lila, do you want to smoke some grass?"

She liked the way Emily said *grass*, an old-fashioned word. They sat and talked about performing and traveling. Then Lila needed cigarettes but was afraid, in a way, to go out, because that might mean the discussion was over. She took the risk anyway, all high and everything, and when she came back, Emily suggested they go to the apartment where she was house-sitting so she could feed the cats.

The walk was misty, quiet. So calm, it had to be a movie set. They were quiet together and Lila liked that. Then Emily babbled things, the kind of things you babble when you're high, and she wasn't embarrassed. Lila liked that too.

"Emily, look at that woman in the gelatti store. The one with her hair dyed black and bleached blonde on top. She's an Italian lesbian named Tina. You lived in Italy, right? You might want to meet her. She's real pretty. Some of my friends told me about her. They're going in for gelatti three times a day just to make conversation. Want to stop and say hi?"

"No thanks. You can if you want to. I'll wait outside."

Lila was embarrassed again. She had invited someone into her fantasy and they had refused.

"I'm sorry, I guess that sounds sort of coarse. I don't know what I'm talking about. I'm just high. Forget I ever said it."

But Emily saved the moment with a wide smile and Lila felt her body dip into the warm breeze filling the space between them. This was a friend.

In a tenement on East Fourth Street, on the fourth floor, the window overlooked a silent summer street. Some Black men murmuring, someone playing the drums, a lone bicycle. She was a pretty woman in a small apartment on a hot night.

Their talk was full of memories and associations, comfortable as old friends, but with the excitement of describing themselves to each other for the first time. Eudora Welty, The Allman Brothers, *Giovanni's Room*, Top Cat, reading Dostoyevsky in high school and finding out there were things to think about in life, like how much control you have and when to take it. They talked about woman things too. About rape, about abortion, about being straight.

"When I lived in Europe I went out with men a few times, but I decided to wait until I met lesbians."

This was a women who waits.

"I liked being straight," she said, "some of it. But, after three months or so I wouldn't want to have sex with them anymore. I would feel repulsed.''

''I haven't touched a penis since 1979,'' Lila told her. ''I do have this one friend though, Sal Paradise. He lives in my building. We hang out together. One night, about a year ago, we were up late in my apartment drinking and talking and I felt so close to him that I wanted to reach out and make love with him but he said no.''

''And now . . . ?''

''Now we get along fine. What the fuck. People want to sleep with each other at different times for different reasons. It's no secret. It doesn't have to poison everything.''

First Emily sat across the floor from Lila and then she sat next to her. Lila brushed some ashes off Emily's leg without thinking. She liked her. She felt like her friend. She wouldn't have minded curling up with her and kissing, but not for romance. She just liked her.

They sat and smoked cigarettes like men do in Hollywood versions of tenement apartments and Lila wondered if Emily was considering kissing her too, or if she was just waiting. Everything felt good and calm. So, Lila, knowing the ways of the grapevine, decided to tell the sad tale of her plans for Helen Hayes, just so Emily wouldn't find out later from someone else. Lila really liked talking to Emily and wanted her to know the truth. She told all the gory details and was genuinely surprised when Emily started laughing out loud.

''You mean you've spent that much time thinking about Helen?''

''Well, it's not like it was the most pressing thing on my mind,'' answered Lila, a bit defensively. ''I just noticed her. Listen, I have lots of crushes all over the place. I just sit back and look at them and think, some of this will come to be and the rest won't, so I'll just enjoy imagining it all for now.

Emily's response was to realize how late it was and how sleepy she was getting, since she had to be at the factory by seven the next morning. Lila put on her shiny shoes and linen jacket and Emily got back to the business of feeding the cats, as if Lila had just stopped by for the rent check, or to deliver a package.

"Come by the Inn and visit."

"I will," Lila said, "I will," and stepped out into the early morning.

THREE

L ila came home feeling all sexy and silky. She sat down at the typewriter and worked until the sun came up. She knew she'd be a wreck in the office, but she didn't care, she wanted to get down every detail of her adventure with Helen Hayes at The Pyramid Club. It was too good a story to lose. She washed her hair, changed her clothes and went down for cigarettes and the mail. There was another rejection letter. This time from a lesbian magazine in southern Pennsylvania. She'd sent them a story about going to the country and getting a crush on a sign-language interpreter for the deaf who she met while hitch-hiking on the back of a pick-up truck. Her intention had been to use their interaction as a metaphor for urban-rural relations. The editors obviously missed the point. Lila re-read their letter three times on the subway to work.

"We like your writing," they said. "You have a wonderful sense of humor. However, there are a few problems with your piece. First, on page one, you refer to *fat* farmers. Why did you have to say they were fat? More important, how do you think fat women will feel reading that word? We also felt this way about page two where you mentioned a *pock-marked local*. We don't want to spout jargon, but who has pock-marked skin? Not rich people. The other thing had to do with the *tiny pink nipples* on page five. If you would not walk up to a woman and say to her face *I think your nipples are a drag*, should you expect us to say it by publishing your story? Thank you for thinking of us and good luck in the future. Signed, The Collective."

As soon as Lila said good morning to her co-workers, sorted the mail and re-filled the xerox machine, she turned on the office's IBM Selectric and wrote back, in one draft.

"Dear Collective,

"I'm sorry that the farmer was fat and that I said so. If only I had said that he was tan instead, that the pock-marked boy was blond and the woman's breasts were like porcelain instead of egg whites with tiny pink nipples. If only I had seen something different than what I saw, or written something different than what I saw, then my work would have appeared in your magazine.

"Either you can let me tell people what I see, or you can decide that they should only know about ways of seeing that aren't anything like fat farmers. Sincerely Yours."

After she mailed the letter, which one always needs to do immediately with letters like that, Lila remembered one of her heroes, Lenny Bruce, and how his solution would have been to climb up on a large billboard somewhere in the state of Pennsylvania and write on it, in careful black letters, fifteen hundred times, *fat farmers*.

FOUR

Work was always there taking up time and rarely meant much short of the postage stolen off the postage meter and the xerox paper stolen for writing and the pens, white-out and xerox copies stolen for Lila's personal use. It was always there and then it was over, leaving her with some kind of need to do something worthwhile, or at least enjoyable, as soon as possible.

She sat in The Cafe Kabul on Saint Mark's Place waiting for someone she needed to see come by, and sure enough, Muriel Kay Starr came walking down the street. She needed to see Lila too, so they walked over to the Futuransky home, stopping off at Punk Chinese for some asparagus to go and saying hello to Tony, a drug dealer on the corner of Ninth and First. He'd probably figured out by this time that Lila and Muriel were lovers.

It took those two women a few years of misunderstanding and unfulfilled expectations to figure out the right way to do it, but eventually they did. Lila was Muriel's permanent affair. It would never be more than that, since everyone knew that Lila Futuransky was not the marrying kind and Muriel, while not ready for the altar, needed to have a primary girlfriend and needed to know where she was every day. Over the years

Muriel's love life had consisted of a series of main lovers, with Lila on the side plus assorted others every now and then. The girlfriends accepted the situation because they knew that Lila wasn't going to take Muriel away from them. From Lila's point of view there weren't many drawbacks except for a few lonely moments now and then when the main girls came first, but she and Muriel could always talk about anything and not worry. Like best teenaged buddies, they would plot together, discuss their problems and usually made love very well, though they didn't mention that fact very often. Once though, Lila did send her a note just to say that Muriel made her cunt feel like butter.

They lay down together on the bed, arms fitting as comfortably as an old, old couch, while Lila read Muriel the story of The Pyramid Club, a copy of which she had just mailed to Helen. Muriel told how she had finally gotten up enough courage to ask out the beautiful Italian woman, Tina, who worked in the gelatti store, even though Roberta, Muriel's main girlfriend of the moment, did not think she was ready to put up with another of Muriel's flings. Maybe Tina would take her off someplace too beautiful, like Brazil. She was ready for anything, as long as it was new.

That seemed to be the latest theme around town. Everyone was looking for something new. Not that the old thing wasn't working out, but just for the sake of change. It all had to do with the weather. First it was cold, freezing cold for months and very private with never enough heat. Then, one day, quite unexpectedly, spring came. People's minds were splitting open right there on the sidewalk, stretching, trying to take in all the images rushing by, trying to synthesize them into some kind of sense. It had to do with the sudden appearance of countless astounding colors combined with having your skin feel the air again. Everyone was out on the street with something to say, giving in to the desire to just emote for a while. But, before anyone had time to get ready, it was summer, and heavy and humid and dark with heat, promising nothing but the same for three months. At that point, each person who still had it within themselves to dream, dreamed. Each person who still believed that those dreams could come to be, started to plot about how they were going to get the hell out of there and get to something new before the heat set in.

This time, though, Lila was thinking she might just go with it, stay and sweat. They say New York dies in the summer, but everyone's still there. It must be the haze rising from the concrete that makes it go private again. But, what if she just stayed with it this time? Somewhere along the line she knew there'd be girls, visions and everything.

FIVE

Muriel called to tell all about her night with Tina. It sounded really nice over the phone to Lila, who was spread out on the floor looking at the big dark tree hanging over her window. It was that exciting warm, cool, fucking weather. She could mess around at home or go out looking for something. What was there to read anyhow? *The Trial? Portnoy's Complaint?* No, four times was enough. *On the Road?* Lila often asked herself why she tried to write lesbian fiction when she never read any. She had a lifetime of stories piled up in cardboard boxes over her desk. Someday they'd all come crashing down on her head. She could see the New York Post headline: BRUNETTE BURIED BY UNPUBLISHED MANUSCRIPTS.

A writer who never published anything had a hard time convincing other people that she was really working. Take Emily, for example. Anyone could walk into The Kitsch-Inn and there she would be, covered in paint, scraps of material all over the floor. Even if no one knew exactly what she was doing, they could be sure it was something. As for Lila, she thought of her ideas alone, wrote them down alone, took them to the post office alone and got back the rejection letters alone. The only evidence were those goddamn cardboard boxes. The other problem was that, lately, Lila had been writing faster than she had been living and sooner or later was bound to run out of material. Maybe she should read *On the Road* again. Only, from a different angle this time. The trick was to identify with Jack Kerouac instead of with the women he fucks along the way. She could easily get into his kind of head. Everyone else just sits around, but Jack *does* it! No grass grows under his feet.

But the night was too clear to waste, so, she stuffed Jack into her back pocket and jumped out onto the street, heading towards Sally Liberty's garden over on East Sixth. On her way she ran into Isabel Schwartz in her purple jacket and purple sneakers, just coming home from her waitressing shift. She was talking to herself very intently and wheeling her purple bicycle. There's an expression, *two Jews, three opinions,* and lesbians are exactly the same way. So, although Isabel Schwartz was also a drama dyke, she was coming from a completely different school of thought than the Kitsch-Inn crowd.

"Miss Schwartz, you look like you've got something interesting turning over in your brain."

"Miss Subways, yes, I've got an idea for a new show."

Isabel always called Lila "Miss Subways" because she said it was an appropriate name for a soon-to-be underground hero.

Isabel Schwartz worked forty hours a week slinging burgers and saving her quarters until she had enough to put on a show. Her plays were tales of average lesbians and the little things they knew and cared about. Then it was back to the burgers.

"It's going to be called *Job Revisited,* about God and the Devil and there is no good and evil, but they keep tempting me with promises of love and success. I haven't got it all figured out yet, but what I do know so far is that, in the first scene, the Devil will be a rabbi and God will be my mother. In the second scene, the Devil will be my mother and God will be the rabbi. Finally, in the last scene, they'll both be my mother."

"What is your mother going to say about all of this?"

"She loves it. I've done nine shows, each one about my mother, and she loves them all. Except the one before last where I killed her. She didn't like that one."

Once Isabel and Lila went to an off-Broadway theatre to see what shows were like when you paid twenty-five dollars for a ticket. The piece was by a playwright from Missouri, with actors from Chicago and an audience from New Jersey. All were pretending that they were dramatically interpreting the reality of New York street life. The actors strutted around, jiving like bad imitations of Eddie Murphy imitating a Black teenager imitating what he saw Eddie Murphy do on TV the night before. The lesbian characters kissed each other and hit each other. The gay male characters made jokes about the sizes of each other's penises. The Black characters ran around with afropicks in their pockets and occasionally stopped combing their hair long enough to play three-card monte while saying "motha-fucka" a lot and grabbing their own crotches. All of this provided an appropriately colorful background for the white heterosexual characters to expose their deeply complex emotional lives.

"You know what gets me the most," Isabel said after they walked a few blocks home in silence. "Everyone runs around complaining that New Yorkers control the world. But it's not the people who really live here. It's the ones who came from somewhere else, you know, like Americans."

Lila nodded her head, paying close attention to the way Isabel had of figuring out what was really going on.

"Then, after they're here a while, they write these plays and books and songs about what it was like coming here from somewhere else. As if this was a city full of golden angels getting off the Greyhound bus with a suitcase full of dreams battling their way past the local slugs until they get to their righteously deserved pot of gold."

"Yeah Miss Schwartz, I know what you mean. Like Dustin Hoffman, or someone like him, who grows three days' worth of beard, grunts and thinks that means he's playing a real person. He hasn't been one for so long that he can't see the difference."

"That's called fake social realism," Isabel said, and a new category was born.

SIX

Lila turned down Sixth Street to Avenue B. Once she got past all those stupid art galleries, it was still a nice block. With the creepy, crawling invasion of gentrification into the neighborhood, it was becoming harder and harder to find a quiet street. Things were so bad that even Avenue A was unlivable. The Good Humor man had been replaced by tofutti-selling teenaged boys in teased Mohawks. Polish and Puerto Rican mom and pop soda foundations featuring Breyer's ice cream, vanilla or chocolate, bowed to the pressure of imported ices. Tanned Europeans in skimpy t-shirts sold one dollar and fifty cent scoops-du-jour. But, over by Avenue B there was still life on Sixth Street. Lila passed an old Irish bar with a pool table, a few bodegas and the combination Jesse Jackson for President campaign headquarters and thrift shop, until she got to the former vacant lot on the corner. For years it was full of garbage and served as a shooting gallery for junkies, but that night, in the dark, Lila could make out three silhouettes laughing and talking in the rubble. Sally Liberty, Lacy Burns and, surprise, Muriel too, looking pretty as usual. The real surprise though, was that once she climbed over all the bricks and things, Lila stumbled into a few little gardens, here and there, with mari-

golds and tomato plants. Just little patches where Sally, a short
white woman from West Virginia and Lacy, a tall Black woman
from Queens, had gone out with pick axes and lemonade, digging up little sections of the dead earth and bringing it back to
life again. At night they hung out in their gardens with their
kids and lovers and friends, spending the hours telling tall tales.

"Lila, have some wine." Lacy took out another paper cup.

"What's the occasion?"

"Sally's taking off for California on Monday in her big green
school bus, so we're having a farewell party."

"Plus," Sally added, "Lacy is getting another book
published."

Lacy had that look of embarrassment that meant there had
been too much talk already about a real accomplishment and
since she wanted to keep all her friends, she changed the subject as graciously as possible.

"Enough ladies, we are here to enjoy the garden. Lila, you
come by for a visit next week and I'll tell you all about it."

Lacy leaned back, the shadow of a marigold hanging over her
shoulder.

"You bet. Hi Muriel."

She was all curled up, glowing from the heat and a joint, looking up at the empty buildings to the south and the remodeled
ones to the north.

"Sally, have you gotten the bus in shape for the Rainbow
Gathering?"

"We're all set, except for the garden."

"Why? It looks wonderful to me."

"It looks great to me too," she answered. "That's the
problem."

Sally was in her forties somewhere and thought like a Yippie,
which meant giving away food for free, helping out retarded
kids at the Special Olympics and going on The World Cannabis
March. She had lines in her face from a little too much party.
Lila found herself easily seduced by that kind of attitude, so she
always stayed two steps away.

"You won't believe what's been going on around here. The other day, me and Lacy were putting down some dirt and this lady walked up in brand new blue jeans and told us that the City of New York is so proud of our garden that they have decided to adopt it into The Green Apple Program. She handed us a little plaque of a green apple and then told us she was our official organizer."

"But you don't need an organizer," Lila said, "you're already organized."

"That's the truth," Sally nodded. "Then, last Friday, this woman came back and announced that from now on all the gardens had to be square and ours is round. So, she demanded that we take it apart and make it square."

Muriel lay back quietly while the rest really got into shooting the shit and getting blown away by the stupidity of things.

"Look around you," Lacy said, "there's thousands of abandoned apartments and people with no homes and all the city cares about is our garden. They called a meeting and we went. We made a proposal that said we could keep our garden round. That lady just happened to be the one taking the minutes and first she wrote it down and then she crossed it out because she didn't like it. So, Sally starts screaming. . ."

"Yeah, I was so pissed off, I started screaming, YOU FAS-CISTS, ONLY FASCISTS MAKE PEOPLE HAVE SQUARE GARDENS. Then I told them, YOU CROSS ME OUT, I CROSS YOU OUT, and I tore up the minutes."

"But they kept saying THE PLAN, THE PLAN and. . . well, you know how I get around the bureaucratic unimagination," Lacy smiled, "I stood up, very properly and then screamed at the top of my lungs, FUCK THE PLAN, and tore that up too. We hope they'll stay away but with the city, you never know. We'll be out here a lot this summer, me and Arthur and Kwame, holding down the fort while Sally's on the coast."

Everyone got quiet then, like they all ran out of breath at the same moment and sat back, satisfied at having told a good story.

"I'll be here all summer too," Muriel said.
"I guess we all will be."
Then there was a quiet breeze.

SEVEN

L ila's mind kept drifting back to Emily Harrison and the good feelings that had passed between them. A few times she considered going over to The Inn to pay a call. The only problem was avoiding Helen Hayes, who also hung out there. On the other hand, maybe she should get the humiliation over with and just show her face before she lost it. Maybe not. But, to be sure, she climbed the fence in front of a lot down the block and made her way over a whole alley's worth of garbage and rusty bed springs to peek in through the back window. Yep, the lights were still on. Something was happening, but she couldn't bring herself to knock on the window. Lila guessed she'd been a little bold before and had gone too far. Now she was feeling some timidity on the rebound and wanted to avoid looking like an asshole at all costs. So, she walked the streets for a little while longer.

Lila cruised First Avenue between Seventh Street and Tenth Street quite often in the course of her daily life and every time she ran into three men: Ray, Tony and Solomon. Each one had their own personal story but they were also part of the same old story of men hanging out, just hanging out.

Ray was her favorite. The other dealers called him the old

man because his beard was almost grey, but, at age fifty, he was in better shape than most of the young junkies who worked that strip, with his shiny black skin, his cool beret and tight t-shirts to show off his pretty muscles. Ray had been around, of course. He had organized for The Black Panthers at Wayne State and somehow ended up selling nickel bags in the East Village. He had a girlfriend for a while, a white woman named Asia. But after her kid was born she split and went back to North Dakota where she knew Ray would never follow.

One night Lila and Muriel were drunk and dancing and teasing the slam dancers who had just started coming around the neighborhood. They didn't have their own bar at that time so they hung out occasionally at The Park Inn where there was some Hard Core on the juke box and drafts were still seventy-five cents. A little after midnight Ray stepped in for a break, looking sharp as always and needing some company. Well, he liked Muriel right away, with those aquamarine eyes, and she was in a party mood.

"Ray," she smiled, genuinely happy to see him. "Ray, come see my new dance piece. It's a love story about two women, it's really romantic, you'll love it." With that, she threw her arms around his pretty neck.

"Uh. . . Muriel, Ray and I haven't exactly talked this through yet."

"Yeah," he said, looking around to make sure no one he knew was listening. "But I got eyes, Lila. You know I'm not what you'd call an unobservant guy. I see everything that happens in this neighborhood. Listen, I've been around this kind of thing before. It doesn't bother me. No problem. You know what I'm saying? No problem at all. I meet all kinds, all kinds. No problem."

She began to wonder if there might be a problem.

But the evening ended happily after some more beer and Perrier for Ray who, like a lot of dealers, never touched alcohol. Muriel gave him two free passes, though he showed up by himself. Ray sat quietly through the whole thing, even the part where Muriel made out with another woman on stage.

"You tell it how it is from your perspective," he said later under the flashing DON'T WALK sign, "and that's the only way that you can tell it."

So Ray was cool in Lila's book. That's why, one night, when he ran up to her and asked for twenty bucks, she said sure. In three years the guy had never done her wrong. She gave him the twenty bucks and the next thing she knew, the man disappeared. At first she was pissed off. Ray, why fuck up a friendship for twenty bucks? She checked out all his spots, Bryant Park, the west side of Washington Square, but no trace. Finally, after three weeks, she was riding her bike in Chelsea and a voice called out, "Lila, hey Lila." It was Ray.

"I've been laying low," he said. "You know I got into that cocaine and it started to kick my ass. It's costing me around two hundred and fifty dollars a day. I could have gone to the Virgin Islands. I could have gone to Hawaii. I've been chasing that cocaine like I never chased any woman. Finally I decided to get me some, you know, counseling. I got in touch with a center over here and I'm trying to stay away from those old places."

Good old Ray. She wished him luck, told him to postpone the loan until he got his shit together and rode off into the car exhaust of Eighth Avenue. About three days later, Lila got up to go to work and who did she see back on the corner but Ray, high as a kite, selling those nickel bags. From then on the pattern was set. He'd be standing around selling tiny bags of bad pot to cars with New Jersey plates or kids who hung around in front of the punk bars. As soon as he had enough cash to fill his freebase pipe, Ray would flag a cab, go off somewhere and be back about an hour later selling again. Lila worried about that man but there was nothing she could do. She could spend her life trying to save Ray, but it wouldn't work. She knew it would never work.

EIGHT

Then there was Tony, a young Puerto Rican guy from Tenth Street.

"Lend me five bucks," he said.

"No Tony, I'm not handing out any more money."

"Come on, just five. That way I can buy a bag and sell it for ten. With five bucks I can make a hundred."

"No man, I lent money to Ray and until I get it back I'm not lending out any more."

"That old man, he touches everyone. He only got twenty out of you because he knows that's all you're worth. If you had any kind of bucks at all he would have touched you for a hundred."

Tony slurped his Seven-Up.

"I'm getting sick of hanging out," he said. "I'm gonna take the civil service exam."

"What kind of civil service?"

"Correctional officer. I haven't got a record, or anything."

"Sounds great."

Tony was too skinny. He used to be good-looking but his eyes got too hollow. Besides, he developed a terrible twitch from looking out of one side of his face and talking out of the other.

"Hey Lila, you want to go out with me sometime? For dinner

or something? We can go eat, what's that called, lobster."

"I don't think so Tony."

"Why not?"

"I just don't think so."

"You got a boyfriend or something?"

"No."

"What's the matter, you don't like guys? You a lesbian or something?"

"Yeah, I'm a lesbian, but I'm friendly."

She didn't want this man to become a problem. You've got to stay on someone's good side if you're going to see them thirty-seven times a day. Anyway, Tony already knew that Lila was gay, he just forgot.

They'd met about two years before when Lila and her faggot friend Elliot decided they wanted to make an office space for lesbian and gay writers in the East Village where lesbian and gay writers had always flourished but never had an office. They contacted a housing organization called East Village Independent Livers and got introduced to Mark, a young, white nerdy guy who had just gotten out of college and wanted to become a "community activist."

"I'm Mark," he said. "I'm your organizer. I personally have nothing against homosexuals, but I don't think that the other people involved in this building project would want to work with you. They're all Third World."

"Why don't you let us talk to them?"

"No," said Mark, "I'm sure it wouldn't work. They're concerned with real survival issues."

At any rate, Elliot and Lila, using all the survival tricks they'd learned from years of queerness, wormed their way into the group and found out that it consisted of two Puerto Rican dykes who were lovers, a Black gay guy named Craig, a little guy named Fred, who was also Black, lived in the men's shelter and said he went "both ways," and Tony.

The building they were squatting in had been sitting abandoned for years. Each apartment had been lived in until the tenant died and in most cases, no one had ever come by to take away their stuff. So, each unit was packed with all the belongings of a person's entire life, from clothes to photographs to pots and pans. Only, it had all been tangled up and trashed by junkies and was covered with human shit and blood and used works. The hallways were full of garbage and broken down refrigerators. The grand finale, however, was the top floor. Some weird artist had lived there and filled one room from floor to ceiling with dirt and another room from floor to ceiling with hay. It took all of them and all of their friends about three hundred hours of physically hauling the stuff out before the place got cleaned up. They'd be there sweating while, every so often, Mark would stop by to say, "You're doing a great job, but we've got to keep on working."

"What do you mean *we*, white man," Fred would murmur under his breath.

On the last day everyone carried out about eight hundred filled plastic garbage bags while Mark spent the entire time fiddling with the lock on the front door. Finally one of the friends of friends went up to him and asked, with sweat pouring down her face, "What are you doing?"

"I'm the organizer here," he said.

The next day when everyone was ready to move in, they showed up at the building with all their stuff at ten in the morning and, coincidentally, the cops were there too, with a big strange lock on the door.

"What's going on?" Tony demanded.

They didn't get the full story until some weeks after, even though they could all see the landlord moving in hordes of rich bitch tenants into their nice, clean apartments. Tony filled Lila in on the details one slow afternoon on the corner, while chewing on a fried plantain chip.

"It was that turkey Mark," he said, looking around, as always, for customers and cops. "He was fighting with his girlfriend and bragging to her about screwing one of those girls from PR, just to make her jealous. You know it was bullshit to make her jealous."

"Yeah," nodded Lila, knowingly.

"The girlfriend, who didn't have it all together upstairs since she was going with a jerk like that in the first place, wanted revenge, so she called the cops saying we was using needles in that building. They called the landlord and next thing you know, the people were back on the street."

He crumpled up the empty bag and tossed it under the car.

"Mark's still got that job, Fred's back in the shelter and you and me got nothing better to do than stand here and make conversation with each other. Haven't heard much about the girlfriend though."

Just then a patrol car turned the corner and Tony disappeared into Mercedita's bodega pretending he was buying a Seven-Up. Lila waited a few minutes till the cops pulled away, and was about to get going herself, when out of the corner of her eye she saw Ray flag down a cab.

NINE

Finally, there was Solomon. He was a different breed. Solomon was a hard working boozer in a dirty stetson who hung out on the stoop drinking vodka out of a paper bag. He was always willing to show a photo of his ex-wife in Haifa with their kids. Sometimes Solomon had a carton of Players cigarettes for five bucks. Usually, though, he was just working every day on the block, loading and unloading for a wholesale Italian grocer. The store's thirty-five years of business was about to end that summer when the lease expired and the rent would get jacked up so high only an art gallery could afford it.

After the changes in the neighborhood had started getting really dramatic, this new organization suddenly made itself known. The Concerned Neighbors for a Cleaner Block. Usually block associations were good, helping everyone get to know each other, planting trees, getting a new street light. But this one had a bad feeling about it. First they put up posters of a young white couple walking fearfully down a city street filled with menacing jungle animals, like baboons. The caption read "Clean Up Our Street." It hadn't taken Lila very long to realize that any group of people who wanted to "clean up" another group of people were usually bad news. With long-time tenants getting evicted left and right, all these people cared about was the drug dealers selling nickel bags. It bothered them. Of course, they all did drugs themselves, especially cocaine, but they did it in their apartments. The dealers were selling on the streets and that's what they didn't like. They couldn't claim it was bad for children, cause most of the children on that block had been evicted a long time before. Developers liked to tear out six apartments filled with kids and put in one luxury duplex for some kind of rich artist. Lila had seen the photos on TV. One day, she'd noted four of those posters within five feet of each other and almost bumped right into Solomon. He looked real bad, confused, like he had three hangovers at once.

"Lila, I have had bad times, bad times. I was working in front of the store last week. It's been hard work packing up thirty-five years of stuff. I was on my break when this little lady comes up to me asking if she can buy a nickel bag. I'm sitting on the olive oil and I said to her, *I don't sell no nickel bags. If that's what you want, ask him,* and I pointed to Tony. Do you know what?" He paused, leaning back on his hips, so that he towered over Lila, standing straight with an expression of pure disbelief in his eye. "Do you know what? She was a cop and she gone and arrested me then and there for accessory to a sale. I been in jail for three days now, no cigarettes or anything. Shit."

Lila called up the president of the Concerned Citizens and gave him a piece of her mind.

"You bleeding heart," he said, "You're living in the past. Do you want this street to be taken over by drugs?"

"I like drugs, I use drugs. Anyway, you can't go around arresting every Black person who walks down the block."

"Listen Lila Futuransky, I'm sick of your sixties-esque posturing. Just look out your window and you'll see that you're too late."

He was right. There were two policemen on *horseback* clip-clopping merrily along.

"Don't tell me you called in the Cossacks. Does this mean we're occupied?"

"Yup."

"Well, just think about this," she said. "When there are too many drug dealers, you call in the cops. But who are you going to call in when there are too many cops?"

Solomon had seen many hard days in his life and expected to see many more, so he soon settled back into his spot on the steps, drinking vodka out of a paper bag.

Ray, Tony and Solomon. Some of the men in Lila's life. She spoke to those guys more often than she spoke to her family, or any lover.

Speaking of which, she still had that Emily Harrison on the brain. Lila smiled at the thought of seeing her again. She firmly resolved to swallow some pride and check out The Inn one more time. But, it was too late. The door was all locked up. All the girls had gone to sleep. Still, Lila was buzzed and overflowing with street fever.

If she had been Jack Kerouac, she would have run right over to that apartment on Fourth Street where Emily was staying, climbed in through the fire escape and whisked her off on the F train to Brighton Beach, where, after hours of beer and all kinds of good talk and smoke, they would make love on the dirty sand when the sun came up. Or she would spend all night on the stoop, digging the Eastside night life, smoking cigarettes and tripping until the morning when Emily just might come down for a quart of milk and there she would be, disheveled and grinning. They would walk down to the water in the early morning cool, two women with bare shoulders, walking side by side, talking quietly as women have been known to do.

TEN

Bored again. Jack Kerouac had already gone through twenty-eight pages without having sex with anyone. He hadn't done anything substantial either, but he'd had a sensational time doing it. Lila was bouncing up and down the stairs, looking for fun on the Saturday afternoon of Memorial Day weekend. Every now and then she would stop in front of the mirror to say "Four more years of Ronald Reagan," realizing that that fact was a large part of how apocalyptic things felt lately. Then she'd go back on the street with Solomon, who had been trying to sell homemade leather belts to weekend tourists before the rain started. The afternoon got late and Lila took a few deep breaths to get her courage together before the start of whatever came next.

Then, just like the beginning of every night, the question got answered when someone familiar walked by, coincidentally at the very moment she needed to see him. There was Sal Paradise, looking pretty with his ponytail and clean-shaven face.

"Sal," and Lila was so happy to see him, and he was happy to see her too, because they both knew they could get down to brother-sister talk, have some beers and go anywhere.

"What happened to your beard?"

"I decided to come clean for Gene."

"Wishful thinking."

The rain broke as they ran into an old Polish bar on Seventh Street.

"I've been working ten hours a day on construction over at Thirty-Eighth and Eleventh. The boss is paying five hundred dollars a week in cash to create a completely electronic garage, installing luxury gadgets in limousines. The neighborhood is scuzzy as shit. I'm always seeing prostitutes and sometimes they're getting beaten up by their pimps. We're busy working on limos and don't do anything about it when we hear them yelling out for help. I just feel sick and don't say anything. I'm there for the money. One guy on the job has five thousand dollars hidden under his mattress. There are women who are so used up they have nothing left to sell. They go out into a lot with some pretty dirty men and do what they can for literally a couple of bucks. The others guys call out for me to come watch, but I just keep working on those limos. Yesterday I had this one that was so full of crap, we couldn't even install our gadget. It had a TV and a bar and a stereo and a telephone and those shaded windows. Someone is very ill to need all that."

The storm part ended and was followed by soft, warm drops, steady and harmless. They didn't care, and walked, all wet, over to Sally Liberty and Lacy's garden, but they weren't hanging out. Then Sal and Lila checked out a building on Thirteenth and A that was supposedly falling down. The whole street was blocked off with police cars and sawhorses. Puerto Rican families were sitting around on their stoops in the rain, drinking Miller beer, smoking Marlboros and watching the building, waiting for it to collapse. Lila and Sal smelled the sweet grass of Tompkins Square Park and sat in a pew at Saint Brigid's on Avenue B.

"Catholics always have the biggest churches," Lila whispered.

"That's because they have the best quality slaves to build them."

They started walking again, blending in with the muted colors, faded denim against the washed-out red of tenement buildings that had been really lived in.

"Sal, how's your sax going? I love coming home at night and hearing you play slower versions of Coltrane solos. Sometimes I just stand on the stairs and listen for a while. I haven't heard anything the last few weeks though."

"It's the job, it takes over everything. First I was coming home and writing poems about it. Now, I just can't, I'm so exhausted. Lila, I slept with a man again. That makes twice in ten years. I feel a little shy about it, but I do know I like sucking cock. I guess I can tell you that."

There were so many feelings going around at the same time. There was the global plane, where, frankly, things looked bad and no one wanted to face it. Like the neighborhood changing. Everyone knew it was going to happen and then that it was happening. Now it had finally happened. Just like the grotesque certainty of Ronald Reagan's re-election, no one could really accept how much more cruelty they'd have to see. But summer also brought new dimensions of feeling on the street, with different kinds of love and sex for each person. You saw someone and you wanted to touch them because you loved them, or because you didn't know them and they're pretty. Because they had a way of wearing an earring, or turning and smiling, or special long fingers. Your heart would just melt for that second and you'd want to kiss her breasts or suck his cock, the way Sal did. The air was murky and thick enough to hide anybody's shyness. Because, even when the shit is hitting the fan, people can still have good times.

Lila told Sal about Helen Hayes and about sending her the story of their evening with no response yet. About Emily Harrison too. About how Lila saw a woman and wanted to touch her, but it wasn't happening that way, so now, everything was unknown.

"But what the hell, Lila, go for it. She's already given you something special, even if she doesn't know about it."

Lila knew that he was right.

They swung back towards their building until she decided to go off in search of more girls, so Lila and Sal gave each other big hugs, boy and girl hugs. She remembered how some men have those muscle arms and you don't realize how much bigger they are until you get hugged.

"So Lila, when are we going to have an affair?"

Oh, yes, her words to Helen coming back to her like a gift. Just a little present to let her know she was not the only one searching out the company and the stimulation.

"One of these days."

She was ready again, refueled, and headed off to Lacy's apartment with a smile on her face. When there was no one home, she just left a note "Hi L, I will return," not knowing if it was true or not. Then back towards the Kitsch-Inn where she saw Emily sitting on the stoop quietly reading a book.

ELEVEN

E mily sat there with those same green eyes and thirty-some-thing-year-old face, kind of like some actress somewhere. Lila leaped up onto the stoop next to her and started reciting from Jack.

"In their eyes I would be strange and ragged and like the prophet who walked across the land to bring the dark word and the only word I had was wow."

Then, in a swashbuckling mode, Lila invited her to the garden, which was the most romantic place she knew, but Emily didn't feel like entering strange territory, no matter how cool. So, they ended up on Sixth Street on another stoop, smoking joints and cigarettes and talking more about Emily's life. She talked about her constant travels all over the world, about her theatre work, about her jobs.

"I usually work in factories, sewing, printing, whatever's there. That way I can get materials for costumes and sets. Stage design? It's basically a matter of extending other people's ideas, making them look good. I want every detail to be perfect. Someone else decides what it's all about and then I decorate it, compensating for a weak script or a bad actress with a dazzling effect. When the audience walks in, I want them to take one look and gasp."

Lila paid attention. She was gathering information but didn't know how to put it all together. Instead she just watched the different expressions Emily's face was capable of. Sometimes she seemed like a dress-for-success executive whose bra was held together with staples. Then she became a silly girl sitting over a Tab in a coffee shop. Lila began to wonder, was she courting this woman, or were they just making friends?

They walked into a late night bookshop and stood quietly looking at a map of the world.

"I used to live here," Emily said, pointing to a spot on the page. "When I look at it I get so excited. I can hear the voices of my friends and remember the clove and dried flowers. Watch it shiver, reverberating off the paper."

Lila looked at the map, trying to decide where to go. It occurred to her that since the time of maps, people have been able to look upon other countries as empty pink and green shapes. Furthermore, Lila noted each country's maps projected different interpretations of size, boundary and centrality. Basically, though, Lila concluded, a map's first purpose was to state that the most important division in life was geographical.

They walked some more, not knowing exactly where until Emily suggested stopping for a beer. But, when they got to the bar, she expected Lila to pay, and then asked her if she played pool. Second thoughts began to present themselves. Maybe, Lila worried, this woman with a mysterious past was a pool shark. That would be interesting. To try to win the heart of a con-artist without losing your shirt. People who travel all the time are weird anyway, she thought. They spend most of their energy having introductory conversations and brief romances without going through anything with anybody. Their lives become focused on scoring a place to sleep and finding a job until the next train. Lila nursed her beer for hours but still couldn't get Emily to mention the name of any lover she'd ever had, even though they sat in that bar till way past midnight.

Emily decided to go home even though Lila could have

walked the streets with her all night. As the morning started to come their way, they passed by the locked up Inn and Lila saw, sticking out from under the door, the very letter she had sent to Helen Hayes with her story. Helen had never received it. Lila took that as an omen that she was on the right path and put the letter in her pocket. When the moment came to say good-bye, Emily started to run off, but Lila put her arms out for a hug and Emily kissed her instead and said it again.

"Stop by the Inn sometime."

As usual, Lila didn't know what she meant but felt freer somehow with that letter in her pocket.

It had only started on Monday, but already everything had come back full circle. There were still two days left to Memorial Day Weekend and time for another cycle to start and come to fruition. Or maybe everything would just sit there for a while and inspire Lila to move on to other adventures. That night, finally in bed, she lay with her shirt off, in her underwear and blue jeans, like Jack on his bunk, looking out on the shadows of the rooftops and doorways, watching the streetlight shine on her flat stomach. Lila listened to the trees tremble, getting ready for whatever came next.

PART TWO

TWELVE

"The arty types were all over America sucking its blood," said Jack Kerouac to Carlo Marx in Denver. From Lila's East Village vantage point, she could see that he was right. At least as pertained to the ART SCENE which was oozing its slime all over Second Avenue. The upscale New Yorkers who cabbed it down to the fancy spaces to see performers on tour from Europe, ate out afterwards in restaurants where Lila couldn't even get a job. It was an invading homogenous monster composed of a lot of boring people thinking they were leading wacky lives. Lila was beginning to regret her haircut.

Unfortunately the scene was getting older and more established and Lila had begun to watch its participants change fashions and pretensions as they passed her in the street year after year. From lots of overheard conversations and sterner expressions Lila deduced that as the person aged they'd often stop and take a look at how they'd been spending their art time. Occasionally that brought new insight and change. Usually it meant doing commercials or applying for grants. But for every dropout, there were three new recruits stepping off the commuter train.

Like Linda Kasbah, who had gone through a lot of changes.

She'd started out really wild, actually taking risks, not just dressing like she did. Linda worked nights as a go-go dancer in New Jersey for a while, endlessly whizzing by on the back of some guy's motorcycle. Then she got smart, and realized if she go-go'd in pretentious performance spaces and threw in some post-modern movements she could get somewhere, and did. In fact, she ended up with a tour of Europe with her show *Avant Garde A Go-Go* and dropped out of sight for a while, until the day Lila bumped into her in front of Leshko's Polish Restaurant. There was Linda, calm and restrained, standing next to a tall handsome man and pushing a baby carriage.

"This is John," she said, stepping into the frame of a one-celled nuclear family, "and this, is Jane."

Lila tried to be cool, chatting for a bit, inviting Linda over to try out a new idea she'd had, but Linda just nodded her head, and clutched Lila's arm with a ferocious urgency, startlingly tight and imploring.

"A new idea, yes, yes, it's a very different life, Lila, a very different life."

So that was one way out. One could also get thrown out, burned out, or even make it for a while, until the critics and funders who built you up decided it was time to tear you down. Some people never got anywhere but never gave up, clinging to their defeat until they died or got bored.

There was Muriel and her main girlfriend Roberta standing in front of Performance Space 122, wearing little white pinafores.

"What's going on?"

"It's about twenty-four hours," said Roberta looking kind of sleepy as usual. She was wearing her standard flowing robes, in their usual three shades of green, under her pinafore.

"What do you mean?"

"We're in a performance," Muriel sighed. "It's twenty-four hours long."

"What's it about?"

"Twenty-four hours."

"Oh."

"Here Lila," Roberta handed her a pinafore. "We need some more Alices, come on, let's go."

Inside the theatre some very worn out dancers were rolling around glossy-eyed in various states of dance marathon exhaustion. Lila, Muriel and Roberta ran over to a small crowd of women, all dressed in little white pinafores.

"Okay Alices," said the head Alice, "First we enter when he says *coming out of the woods*. Then we line up, then we break."

"What does *break* mean?" Lila asked Roberta.

"It means that after we're on stage and we line up, then you do whatever you want.

Lila decided to pay close attention to the stage activity for the next hour before she went on. The act of the moment was a woman in a thirties bathing suit reading boring postcards that her friends had sent her. Then some people pushed a bowling ball back and forth. After that, a woman who was a very important person to know and a man with a big grant danced with their mouths full of parsley. Finally, Lila could see a pattern emerging. First, you sort of moved around and then you said unrelated things in a deadpan. She could do that. She did that everyday. Suddenly, he said *coming out of the woods* and the Alices lined up and then they broke. Roberta and Lila slid down the middle of the floor and then Roberta said, to no one in particular, "I liked the parsley best."

"I counted. There are more artists than there are ideas to go around," Lila said, rather pleased with herself.

"I still liked the parsley."

This was really easy. Roberta starting jumping, so Lila took out a piece of paper, wrote down her phone number and handed it to a pretty woman in the audience. It was fun, but was it worth twenty-four hours?

THIRTEEN

Muriel and Lila needed a break. They went out in the rain to DiRobertis Italian Coffee Shop for a cup. Muriel was a dancer. She listened to Lila's stories and Lila went to see Muriel dance. Then they talked to each other about it. This was a gift they appreciated more than friendship. During those times they were not emotionally close. It was more about being colleagues. They took each other seriously and exchanged their most productive attention. This was not a dreamy time for come-on's and romantics. It was more like DiRobertis' warm silky coffee on a rainy day, which left them solidly awake with the smell of kitchens in their mouths. Whenever Lila thought about going home, she thought about the places where minds met like Muriel's and hers over coffee.

Talking with Muriel let her in to the head of a person whose concerns were completely different than her own. Dance wasn't Lila's way of seeing, but it was a way, and she was glad to know it was there. Muriel's issue was how to create the highest possible energy. She'd forget about wondering where the money was coming from and, instead, ask herself aesthetic questions about feeling a movement, looking to do this within the realm of some kind of emotion. Still, Lila knew that

Muriel's realm did not yet include anger or sadness. "Sensual and elastic," *The Village Voice* critic said, and she did look beautiful on stage. Even though Lila could see her resisting the effort to bring some feeling to all that grace. So, at that moment, there was no genius, but Lila loved her enough to maintain interest, sitting perpetually in Muriel's first row. This was the mood they were in over a coffee break from twenty-four hours.

"Muriel, I can't believe that you've been at this for an entire night and a half a day. Aren't you exhausted? I mean, I could see staying up if it was interesting or fun, but this. . . it's like LSD with no revelation."

Muriel lit a cigarette.

"Well, I did have a weird experience about eleven hours ago. I was performing a series of experimental dances, using haphazard movement without form. In the first piece I thought that Roberta and I were going into a slow contact, like a tango, and then we started dancing. But, she said *too slow,* so I moved out of the dance. Later, when I asked her why, she said I wasn't dancing *with* her, I was dancing *on* her, but I know that if my dance is refused during the improvisation, I just lose all my concentration."

Lila thought back on this conversation the next evening when she watched Muriel perform at The Dance Theatre Workshop and noticed Tina from the gelatti store, all alone, sitting quietly in the back row. Lila thought, *Wow, beauty and grace certainly take one very far.* She saw that Muriel had love whenever she wanted it and sex whenever she wanted it and someone to talk to in an intelligent way whenever she wanted, and that was too much for any one person. With so much diversion Lila would never be able to do the things that she loved best, like walk the streets for hours with nowhere to go except for where she ended up. She would never have the time to bump into a brand new person and give them her total attention. And with that understanding, she was happy to step out alone into the night's heat.

FOURTEEN

Lila's job was so fucking boring and disruptive and ever-present that she decided to try to write about it as a way of turning the mundane into the allegorical. It didn't seem to bother everyone the way it bothered her. Most people just accepted work. Some even enjoyed it because they had absolutely no idea of what else they could possibly do. Without white-out and collating and requisition forms there would be nothing to talk about over the dinner table during commercials. Lila was straining her imagination, looking for ways to turn these office items into symbols of time wasted and possibilities deferred. Unfortunately the greatest angle on all this had already been taken. It was an episode of *The Avengers* when these secretaries killed their bosses and they were the only ones who could run the company because no one else understood the filing system. The problem though, was that there were no more things like filing systems. Everything was getting computerized by the summer of '84, and it was happening so fast, a social critic could hardly keep up with it. Lila was having a hard time building a plot around a WANG word processor. This realization, in turn, stimulated a long rumination on the poor clerical of the future, trapped in her living room with a screaming baby, an unemployed husband and a radiating personal computer through which her invisible boss could monitor every key stroke.

In order to avoid spiritual meltdown, she gave Muriel a call on the company phone to see if she had any suggestions. Instead, Lila had to leave a message on the electronic secretary Muriel had just purchased, hot, on First Avenue for ten bucks.

"Hi Muriel. I know that you have a career to think of, but when I need to talk to you and I get an answering machine, well, it feels like riding on the commuter train, it's shockingly normal behavior."

Lila's metaphors always got a bit fuzzy when she was depressed.

About twenty minutes later Muriel called back, full of enthusiasm.

"I'm so excited," she said, "I bought my ticket for Madrid. Just me. Roberta is staying in New York. She's too tired to pack. I'm flying out on June 24th..."

"No," Lila said.

"Excuse me?"

"No, you're not. We have a show to do on the twenty-ninth. The Worst Performance Festival. Remember? Muriel?"

But she knew it was already too late. There was absolutely no point in going on about it. There were good things to Muriel and bad things to Muriel and this was one of the worst. She was completely undependable. Lila, on the other hand, if she promised one girl a cup of coffee and another offered her a weekend on a yacht, you know you would find her in the coffee shop, smiling through the grease. *Why should the rich and glamorous get everything?* she asked herself repeatedly in a combination of defiance and sincere wonder. Yet, there was no point in getting angry. The tension began to seep out of her body, trained, by experience, to transform anger into calm. *I'm deflating,* she though, *despite all my desire not to.* For one small and unusual moment, Lila felt sorry for herself.

She resolved to leave the office immediately and search out

some happiness, even though it was only four-thirty. Maybe Vicki the office manager wouldn't notice if she didn't try that one too often. Most importantly, Lila needed a shot of the city, so, after sneaking out the door, promising herself to be more careful in the future, she was right in it again. The buildings created a shining path that led directly to safety and adventure. Sometimes she would just put her head down and whiz right through, being part of the rush and the urgency. Sometimes she leaned back as far as she could until she was outside of it. Then she could enjoy how it was too enormous to explain and, at the same time, one solid thing. Nothing could ever be so beautiful as the city because it was a synthesis of people and objects and it felt every feeling and contained every possibility.

Soon she was ambling down Sixth Street where she found Sally Liberty putting up tie-dyed curtains on her big green school bus. Sally was getting ready to leave that very evening for The Rainbow Gathering. For one Jack Kerouac-second, Lila considered going along too, what the fuck. But then, as she sat on a garbage can, smoking a cigarette and trying to decide what to do, she remembered those other things like having no money, and the chance to enjoy the last days of the neighborhood. Lila knew that New York was closed; once she gave up an apartment she'd never find another one.

"No, goddammit Sally, I'm committed to here."

"Don't worry," Sally said, truly believing it. "There are many ways to fly."

That gave Lila a shot of hope again. She ran home as fast as she could, raced up the stairs and jumped in behind her typewriter like a race-car driver behind the wheel. First you turn it on, then you go. She pushed *on*, placed her hands on the keyboard, felt the electric buzz and started. Without any premeditation she found herself pounding out the story of Emily Harrison, about trying to figure her out and why Lila liked her so much. How Fourth Street radiated every time she passed it because she never forgot for a second that Emily was house-sitting there. It took her along in a flash and a daze until, suddenly, it was the end of the page and she had to wake up, put in another piece of paper and go again.

When Lila was a kid, people were always telling her that there was only one way to be and one way to think about things. It didn't take long for her to figure out that that just wasn't so. Writing had been subjected to the same fabrications. People who think everything through for themselves still write exactly the way their fourth grade teacher told them to. "This is how to use time, this is how to use tense, this is what a sentence is."

But, if anyone had really analyzed it, the way Lila had, they would have seen right away that no one lives or feels or thinks in any consistent tense with subjects and predicates. People dangle their emotional participles all over the place. But, if you go ahead and show them something written just the way they experienced it, all of a sudden it's too scary or strange to comprehend.

The very first things Lila had ever written were for the local *Supermarket News*. That was great practice. There was a given event, say, the price of grapefruits. There was an audience. Her job was to describe the event through the lens of her own personality and writing style. There was no looking around for subject matter, only for description, a task she took very seriously. Did the prices *plummet*, or were they *slashed?* She would ask herself what the item really looked like. How the event really felt. She would shake herself, concentrating, grabbing finally and ecstatically at the one and only word that really said it. Now, though, with fiction, she wanted to write in any manner and about anything simply because she felt like it at that moment. She didn't care if the words were weird, indulgent, pretentious or honestly free. Sometimes Lila just let herself look at a lot of ordinary things in a magnificent way.

FIFTEEN

"It sounds like you're just looking at a lot of things and saying WOW," Lacy said when Lila stopped by, "or OH SHIT, or whatever you would say, Lila Futuransky. Nothing wrong with that. What kind of music do you want to hear?"

"Nothing. Let's listen to the rain."

It had been pouring for three days and the rain was seeping into everything.

Lacy was the only person Lila knew who had really achieved what she had set out to do. Well, maybe that applied to Emily too, only Lila still hadn't figured out what Emily wanted from things, least of all, from her. Lacy had published a whole book of poetry and was about to publish another. Lila wanted to ask her advice about Emily and about writing but she wanted to ask both at the same time.

"Lacy, what happens when you see something or someone, but you see them in a dream and everything in your life becomes a pursuit because you want to be close to beauty, to bring it inside of you? But the thing is, you don't want to change yourself. Can you follow a goal and not get lost?"

Lacy sat back and tucked her chin into her chest, which meant she was thinking it all over very carefully.

The silence scared Lila, because it was too heavy for her to hear the answer that she wanted. So, she changed the subject. "Where's Kwame?"

"Arthur took him to the movies. Every month or so Arthur decides that he wants his son to have exposure to some average American culture so he'll know what people are talking about if he ever crosses Fourteenth Street. That's the theory anyway. So he takes him off to the movies. Halfway through, of course, all the sexism and racism and gratuitous violence get to be too much. Arthur gets disgusted and they have to walk out. Poor Kwame's almost six and he doesn't know that movies are ever over. He thinks they're like the sky, cinematically endless."

Lacy was quiet for a moment, shifting in her seat, the way she always did right before getting to the point.

"I'll tell you the truth Lila, I'm honored to be able to publish and all that. I know few people ever get the chance. On the other hand, there's a lot of sickening components to this process. It often makes me want to spend the rest of my writing career developing handbooks for urban gardeners."

"That's not a bad idea," Lila noted, filing the concept away for later.

"First you spend many years staring at bookshelves thinking how incredible it would be to be up there with your greatest heroes, existing apart from yourself. Then you have ideas. Then, somehow, one day, you actually finish writing them down in a reasonable way you find pleasing. When I finished *Crossing The Border*, I thought *Thank God it's finally over. I actually did it*. But no, no, no and no again. You have to sell it, which can take longer than a lifetime. When it was placed I breathed a sigh of relief until the next phase revealed itself. Prepublication."

Lacy was gesticulating wildly, as though she was a young girl conducting a symphony alone in front of her mother's mirror.

"What's that?" Lila asked, finding out about yet another reality.

"That's a great euphemism for endless screaming over punctuation and *no, it is not okay to have a woman in a bikini on the cover, and no, I will not be marketed as the next Lorraine Hansberry.* They have to compare a Black woman to a Black woman, that's revealing enough, but then they compare a poet to a playwright. The guys in marketing probably looked through a book called *Great Negroes* and the only woman in it was Lorraine Hansberry.

"Anyway, years after you write the thing, it finally comes out and of course you don't like it or agree with hardly any of the things it says, but now you have to sell it, so you run around pretending that you do. The publisher, in the meantime, wants to know when you're going to have another one exactly like the first. Lila, I'm not even rich or famous. Imagine how gross it would be to have a big success. Every famous person who ever talked about the experience described how it ruined their life. But we don't listen to that, do we? No, no, no. We don't listen to that. Arthur, home already?"

"*Indiana Jones and the Temple of Doom,*" Arthur muttered, his fishing hat soaked with rain. "Racist trash."

Kwame followed him into the kitchen, leaving a trail of water.

"See, what did I tell you," Lacy laughed, relaxing again.

"But Lacy, what about the revenge factor?" Lila asked, trying to absorb all this new and troublesome information.

"The what?"

"You know, where you saw the world one way and recorded it that way in defiance of all the people who tried to say it wasn't like that. When you got screwed in life and could punch them out on paper."

"Lila," Lacy said, looking tired for a minute. "I find that any character I try to hit on paper will hit me back ten times harder. And as far as making an impression on the living goes, it's my opinion that you only impress those people who already like you or don't know you and what does that mean? The ones who couldn't stand your ass before are going to like it even less after. Look at my mother."

"Rose?"

"Rose. Here I am, thirty-eight years old. A Black woman with two books of poetry. Something to brag to the neighbors about, right? Well, after the first one she was still bugging me that it wasn't too late to go to law school and make some money. But, I thought for sure with the second one . . ."

"No go?"

Lacy smiled again, though her eyes looked sad. She kept her wine glass full and wrapped her body in an old comforter. They were silent in that quiet damp apartment in the East Village in the rain. They could hear the sounds of Arthur and Kwame getting dinner.

"She said to me *Good thing there are exhibitionists out there to entertain the rest of us. I believe some things should be kept private.* You see, *some things* is momma's code word for S-E-X. But, still trying to win her over, I asked, *Momma, don't you like to read and go to the theatre and listen to music? Aren't you glad people took the risk to make those things?* And she answered, *Exhibitionists. They're all exhibitionists.* No, some people you will never win over no matter what you do."

Kwame walked in eating a banana.

"Mom, that movie hurt my head, it was too big."

"I know baby, I'm sorry."

Satisfied with this response, he wandered back into the kitchen.

"You know Lacy, for years I've been trying to figure out parents, since I've never been one, just had them. But now, I get it. They live their lives and then they want to live yours too. Gives me an idea for a story. Something about parents who only want one thing in the world and that's for their child to fail so that they can prove that they were right all along."

"Finally win the argument once and for all."

"That's right Lacy, that's it."

"Lacy," Arthur called. "Come here and tell me if the melon is ripe."

Lila went over to the stereo to put on some music. Oh-oh, it was a tape player. It had been so long since she had lived with a music machine of any kind that she only experienced the last decade of technological advances in high-fi equipment through contact with new models at other people's houses. She didn't even know which way the tape fit into the little plastic envelope that opened when she pressed *eject*. Then there were arrows pointing back and forth, then double arrows doing the same thing. Little meters lit up green next to a square of red plastic that flashed on and off. All this was in addition to knobs labeled with various vague concepts like *tuning* or *tone*. The tapes were the same way, either so new that Lila had never heard of them or so old that Lila had never heard of them. She turned on the radio.

"What are you thinking about these days Lila?" Lacy asked, offering some cantaloupe.

"It has to do with time and girls and Jack Kerouac. With living in a Jack Kerouac novel and one particular mystery girl but a cast of many regular ones too. Something happens in chapter one which gets into Jack's head and leads him through to chapter five where he understands it. In chapter seven, all is reconsidered again because of some revelation about to present itself. That's what it feels like anyway, but my changes are still in their early stages."

"I get it," Lacy said, bouncing back from her author-like somber air and into a round garden playfulness. "Then in chapter thirteen of *Lila Meets The Subterraneans* you ask some Vision of Cody to send you a letter and pretend to put it in chapter fifteen, but actually throw it away and only in chapter twenty does Dr. Sax call you personally to find out why it wasn't there, you Dharma Bum, you."

And Lila knew she understood.

SIXTEEN

"See Isabel, when Emily was a kid, her parents changed jobs every few years. As a result, by the time she was sixteen, she had an intimate knowledge of most major suburbs in America. When she grew up she kept moving, only across oceans too. By the time she came to New York and the windowless back room at The Kitsch-Inn, she had lived on four continents, working tedious jobs with her hands and eyes, sewing, cutting and dyeing. She made things in large factories and small shops. Emily knows a lot about the difference between cultures as well as the reality of solitude and hard physical labor. But she never learned the mundane responsibilities of consistent, dependable intimacy over time. It's like, her primary relationship is with her own ability to create. I think it's been that way since she was a little girl, making things alone in the various houses she passed through and the hotel rooms in between them. She spent her childhood cutting, gluing, putting together, drawing, planning and imagining because she was, at the same time, enormously gifted and in need of something to buffer her loneliness."

"Listen to me buddy," Isabel Schwartz said in response to Lila's story. "Girls like that, you have to watch out for those girls."

Lila was sitting at the counter of Burger Heaven, hunched over an iced tea, cooling off in the air conditioning and listening to Isabel toss advice over her shoulder as she glided back and forth between the tables and the grill.

"They're not like you or me," she continued on the rebound with a ketchup bottle. "You think you're making friends with them because they tell you to *stop by the Inn*. But it's just part of the trap." Her voice faded away as she delivered a mile-high cheeseburger to a smelly man in the corner. "Oh God," she muttered, swinging by the counter again, "he wants another order of raw onion. Why don't people just stay home?"

Finally things quieted down and Isabel could take a seat on the worn out squeaky stools and drink a coke.

"The next step, that's when they talk about sex. That's all they do, talk, talk, talk. You'll be having these all night sensual conversations and the next thing you know you're sleeping over in her bed. Just sleeping of course. I'm telling you, watch out for those girls."

"How do you know so much?" Lila demanded.

"Miss Subways, those girls, they think they're better. They're broke too but they think they have other options. You don't have a chance buddy, not a chance. I don't mean to rub it in your face but didn't you learn anything from the Helen Hayes fiasco?"

Maybe Isabel's right, Lila thought, stepping out again into a gust of hot air, *maybe she's wrong*. Walking through the putrid air of another stagnant early evening, Lila knew that she could never back down without finding out for sure. The problem was approach. This was the time for a new method. Maybe she should try relaxing and being normal. On that note of inspiration, Lila went right home, ironed her famous blue luau shirt, Tennex'd her hair and donned a pair of mirrored sunglasses. It worked. She felt as though she had a tan. Her fingertips tingling with hope and anticipation, Lila walked slowly over to the Inn, on the thin pretext of going to see the show.

As usual Emily was at the door greeting everyone and smiled

largely when Lila made her entrance.

"Hi darlin'," Emily said in her cute nervous way and Lila felt so happy just being around her, she almost forgot to take a seat so she could work on being relaxed. Lila sat in the back row to get a good view of the real show, the usual assortment of local lesbians who made up the audiences at places like this.

Whenever she was in a roomful of lesbians, Lila fluctuated between two points of view. First, she would have a sentimental rush of feeling, overwhelmed by the beauty and the courage of all these women who had gone through fire and ice just to find each other. Every meeting place, tradition or ritual was built with nothing but their own determination, which kept everything vaguely together. But, a split second later, Lila looked more distantly and the scene would be transformed into a room full of victims. This one had her child taken away, that one got locked up by her parents, that one's girlfriend got queerbashed in front of her and there wasn't a thing she could do about it. It made Lila wonder if they really weren't just a bunch of weirdos hallucinating all this fragile dignity. The fact was, that after almost fifteen years of hard core propaganda and heavy publicity, nobody, outside of lesbians, had bought the line that they were strong, determined survivors. To everyone else they were invisible or pitiful and most straight people were plain glad they weren't queer. Still, thought Lila, if only they could put over a *Black Is Beautiful* line of advertising.

Actually, Lila had often considered the question of marketing lesbian popularity. She looked at other groups of outcasts who had managed to make a name for themselves. The ultimate failures were Communists. In America, they were still at the bottom of the charts. After considering various historical examples, she concluded that the most successful model was that of the Beats. Guys like Jack, William Burroughs and Allen Ginsberg, some of them were smart and had some good ideas and wrote some lasting and inspiring work. Mostly, though, they weren't all the geniuses their reputations implied. The thing was, they had made a phenomenon of themselves. They made themselves into the fashion, each one quoting from the other, building an image based not so much on their work as on the idea that they led interesting lives. Lila firmly believed that was exactly what lesbians needed to do. Why not make heroes out of Isabel Schwartz and Helen Hayes, and make The Kitsch-Inn the new mecca? Let kids from all over America pack their bags, sneak out at night and flock to the East Village to hang out with the lesbians. Soon there'd be lines around the block for the Inn's midnight show bringing those hungry for stimulation flocking to catch the last word in Lesbiana. They'd have magazine covers, syndicated situation comedies, do the lecture circuit, maybe even walk down the street without being afraid. Who knows? In Amerika, anything is theoretically possible. The next time she saw Allen Ginsberg buying cannollis at Veniero's, she would be sure to ask him how he did it.

SEVENTEEN

When the show was over, Lila lingered a bit until Emily finally invited her to come along to a party. They went with Sheena, who had just come back from Krishnaland, and Kitty, two members of the inner sanctum of Kitsch. Everything started to feel good again, happy and young and full of energy. Four fearless dykes out on the Friday night streets of their own turf. Just to prove that it was theirs, Kitty and Sheena started staring down motorists with Jersey plates, giving out dimes to beggars and singing old R&B tunes in loud boisterous voices. Kitty was known around as the prettiest Kitsch girl and everyone's old friend. Lila hadn't seen her hanging out for a while though.

"Where have you been, doll? I haven't seen your face since the Halloween Ball."

"Central Park South."

"Central Park South? What did you do, get a rich girlfriend or something?"

"Yeah. She's got two apartments, a building in the Bronx, a restaurant in the West Village and a little numbers business on the side. You want to hear some gossip? We're breaking up. But not till the end of the summer."

Kitty on Central Park South? She used to walk around with literally one dollar in her pocket and stay at people's houses, sleeping anywhere.

"How's that going to be, back on the edge?"

"I can't wait. Do you know what you have to do to be rich? You have to spend all your time with rich people. You have to do drugs even if you don't feel like it because that's what rich people do. Did you know that?"

"I've heard about it."

"You work all the time and then you have lots of things. I like fun. I'm going back to having fun as soon as the summer's over. I think so anyway, I'm not really sure."

"Groovoid," said Sheena.

They ended up at a party of gentrified straight people. It was in a former tenement apartment that had been *rehabilitated* in the style of an early-modern furniture showcase. The package was complete with built-in bookshelves, track lighting and parquet floors. Whoever lived there had a strange collection of books. An entire shelf was filled with volumes on chess. The next one only contained books about poker.

"What does the guy do who lives here?"

"He writes software," Sheena said, "so that lonely people who have computers can play chess and poker with themselves."

Lila walked out on the patio, which used to be a back alley, and ended up sitting with Emily on the lounge furniture. Emily was eating marinated mushrooms from the buffet table, but Lila was already so full with pretty things and the clear sky coming back after so much rain, that she couldn't eat at all.

"I can say some words in Italian," Lila said, looking for some more common ground. *"Cara mia, mi amore, que bella notte."*

"That's nice."

"I also know *dolce mia* and *va funcullo."*

"No, don't say that." Emily's face was overcome by distaste. "I hate when people say that."

Lila knew it was time to try and change the subject, but she didn't know to what, until out of the blue she realized they were talking about sex, just like Isabel had said they would.

"Emily, do you have any lovers in New York?"

"No, not really," she said, absent-mindedly twisting a short curl with her painted fingers. "There are some women who I'm attracted to physically but they all seem to be matched with someone else. Around the Inn anyway, there aren't very many who are pretty, well, pretty to me. But no, except for a few nights with women I've met at parties or. . . well. . . no."

Lila was swimming in the night. She felt so free that she just said it.

"What about me? Are you attracted to me?"

"Yes. . . well. . . no. . . well."

"A little?"

"I don't really know you, Lila."

Lila had that feeling inside like soft evening and soft skin and soft wind and quiet, muffled street noises. Then there was a silence between them, a growing silence.

"I'm sorry if that was a conversation stopper," Lila said. "I wrote a story about you, for you. I even have a copy at home with your name on it. Sometime you'll have to come over and I'll give it to you. Also, I know there's no shower or hot water at The Inn. When your apartment-sitting is up, if you need a place to wash, you can always use my place."

Then they relaxed and partied around a bit, deciding to ignore the gentrifiers and to hang out in a corner with a Colombian lesbian named Olivia and her variety joints.

"This one is California sensemillia. This one is Thai. This one is Jamaican. Now, which one would you like to sample?"

A few hours later, Emily and Lila and Sheena went over to Maureen's, a neighborhood tavern run by a gruff old Irish dyke. Fats Waller was in the background, leftover Christmas lights on the walls. Emily sat in the foreground, her retro haircut illuminated by the flashing reds and greens. All three of them spun on their bar stools, smiling at the old movie posters and ignoring the old customers. They could have been boys or girls in any forties movie.

Sheena went on for a while about her energy and dyeing her hair blue, but Lila was waiting to be left alone with Emily and she thought Emily was waiting too. Even though the thought of being left alone together so late at night made Lila nervous. Still, it was a pleasurable anxiety somehow. As though they were sharing the same thought without speaking, just sitting quietly at the bar.

The events unraveled in such a way that Lila ended up going back to Fourth Street with Emily via an invitation to "watch TV," though it was well past two o'clock in the morning. She was a little surprised when they got there and Emily actually turned on the set. But, trying to go with the flow, Lila sat down next to her and watched *Soul Train*. She even made some conversation about how surprisingly artificial the dancing was, and ditto for the famous *Soul Train* fashions. They sat next to each other for a long time as ads for Ultra Sheen flashed on the screen. Finally Lila asked,

"Do you feel like kissing?"

She asked it because she wanted to kiss Emily so badly and besides, that was what she thought she had been brought there to do.

"Let's just relax," Emily said, curling up. "I'm feeling sleepy. Maybe I'll feel like kissing later."

In the meantime, with Emily's head on her lap, watching *Soul Train*, Lila touched Emily's skin by the TV light and was filled with feeling at how soft and oily Emily's skin was, especially between the fold in her neck, and how warm her curly hair was under Lila's fingers. Even though she ended up sleeping in Emily's bed that night, like Isabel Schwartz had predicted, she still felt happy the next morning that she had finally, in some small way, touched this woman. It gave her so many nice things to think about the rest of the day. Lila knew once again that life was holy and every minute precious.

EIGHTEEN

"Hello Lila? This is Emily."

"Emily. I'm so glad you called me. I was sitting here thinking about you."

"Oh good. Would you like to go to the movies with me? *Annie Hall* is playing at The Saint Mark's."

"I really would like to but I can't. It's time for The Worst Performance Festival to meet on my roof."

According to Lila, artists were supposed to show that there were other ways of seeing. Putting on a show meant calling people together because you had something to tell them, and that something, thought Lila, should not be the same old thing. In the art world, however, this was not the case. At the same time though a depression culture was rising on the streets. There was better dancing in Washington Square Park by Black boys or Puerto Rican faggots than in any performance space. There was Doo-Wop under the Washington Arch and excellent fusion jazz every night for free on Astor Place.

Noticing these contradictions, some of the girls, like Isabel, Muriel and Lila, decided they'd seen enough stupid performances and wanted to do something about it. They invited Muriel's girlfriend Roberta to come along too because she was starting to bill herself as Roberta La Moll and that looked great on a flyer. That was how The Worst Performance Festival was born. They were having their first planning meeting on Lila's roof that Saturday afternoon.

"The concept is," said Lila, "that we want to look at both sides of what it means to be the worst. Some performers are bad because they're about nothing but the audience loves them because the audience is also about nothing. Other performances are bad because they're really about something but that makes the audience uncomfortable, so they don't like it. That is the dialectic of worst."

"We have to help them understand the aesthetic of the worst performance," Muriel added. "Then they can have some criteria for choosing the best contestant since, frankly, almost anything is interesting for three minutes."

"So, what are the essential components of a bad performance?" Roberta asked.

"Well," answered Isabel Schwartz, "it should be something absolutely no one could ever identify with."

"It should be physically annoying," Lila added.

"It should definitely be inaudible," Muriel said.

"But, you know how people are always doing these self-indulgent things like *Disconnected Movements With Irrelevant Objects* where they make you sit there while they do something like count." Isabel wanted the Festival to be as realistic as possible.

At just that moment, the roof was filled with the startling appearance of brilliant colors in a shocking paisley motif. It was Helen Hayes herself, her bleached blonde hair highlighted by a hot pink blouse and turquoise flowered pants. Helen Hayes was in on the show and worst of the worst was guaranteed. She joined the group sitting together on the roof, getting high and talking about the worst.

"Listen girls," Helen suggested, picking up the vibes immediately, "How about a finale like this? *The next performance will be the greatest moment in experimental history, after which the avant-garde will officially be over. Yes, it's true, everyone who has ever won a National Endowment for the Arts grant will now come on stage and shit.* What do you think?"

That Helen cracked everybody up, so people forgot about the meeting and started running all over the roof, looking out over the downtown part of the city. The tenement rooftops of the nineteenth-century Lower Eastside were clear in the foreground while the steel and glass towers of the twentieth-century stood out, separate, in the dusky background.

"Here Helen," Lila said, when no one else was watching. "Here's a letter I sent you, but it got forwarded to the Kitsch-Inn where I found it again, so I decided to give it to you in person."

Helen opened it right then and there and read about how Lila had thought she was cute and smart but a real bitch. She even laughed out loud at the "I meant to call you" line.

"I'm a real nerd," she said. "I'll be sure to show this to Nancy, my new girlfriend, so she'll know what I passed up."

Lila had been carrying around a message to Helen about warmth and embarassment and being a jerk and leading the kind of life that they both led. Helen understood about uncertainty and experiment and unreasonable expectations. They were trying to do good work, have good sex, make meaningful friends, and do all this with no impetus except their own ambition and desires. There was no support outside of that tiny community of downtown dykes who understood being compelled towards an unlikely goal.

The idea was to keep feelings in circulation but still stay friendly, and it had worked. Everything was fine again. Helen knew she was still in Lila's life, even in a small way. Lila had come through that risk feeling good about herself and the people around her. Lila was on the right path.

NINETEEN

All the girls left except Muriel, since she and Lila hadn't had any time alone for a while. They lay down on a blanket on the roof in the last of the Saturday sun of early June and watched the sky.

"I know you're mad at me for taking off and leaving the festival, Lila."

That was exactly what Lila did not want to talk about.

"But you have to let me make decisions about what is best for me."

"Muriel, while theoretically I may agree with what you say, you always make your decisions based on what is best for you. Sometimes there are other people involved too, you know."

"I just want you to understand that I have to do what is best for me and it is best for me to go to Madrid now while I have the money."

"Muriel, I'm not trying to talk you out of it, but I'm not going to give you approval for it either and that's exactly what you are trying to get out of me."

Lila lay on her back with her hands over her eyes. All this tension was not worth it. She was willing to drop the whole argument. Why did Muriel have to push it too far? Now, how was she going to get out of this so they could be in a good mood again?

Lila looked at Muriel. They didn't look each other in the eye during emotionally intimate moments like fights. They usually talked over the phone or while sitting next to each other in an audience, or side by side walking down a street.

"What are you feeling, Muriel?"

"I don't know." She played with the tar-papered roof. "I'm feeling sort of vulnerable."

And then she cried. First Lila thought it was a trick of some kind because, when it came down to it, she didn't really trust Muriel. But then she realized that she couldn't remember that happening before so, guardedly, she felt for her.

"This weird relationship we have is so important to me, Lila, and I know that at any minute you could get really angry at me and stay away for a long, long time."

How could Lila help but hold her because, somewhere, she also had a need to tell Muriel how important she was to her.

"Muriel, I think if we cared any more for each other than we do we would never get along. It's always when we get really involved that we lock horns."

That felt like the truth. Their eyes met in a silent understanding. Then Muriel leaned in to kiss her. When Lila smelled her smell, she moved towards her with the same force and their emotional and intellectual feelings faded away to be considered another day, replaced by the power of sexual unity. Although the disagreements and conflicts were certainly irresolvable, there was a place of sexual confidence that kept them coming back to each other time after time. Then they sat back out of their kiss and were themselves again with different egos and points of view.

"Why don't we just stay here on the roof?" Muriel said.

Lila started to smooth out the blanket when she saw two men on the next roof staring at them.

"We have to go inside. There are two men staring at us."

They went inside and covered the windows so the men

couldn't see into the apartment. Muriel took off her clothes and Lila took off her clothes. Without any seduction or conversation they put their arms around each other's waists, held each other's asses and pressed their naked bodies against each other. They put their cool hands on each other's hot thighs. Every move was deliberate and strong. Their confidence in each other was so deep that Lila always anticipated the pleasure before it came. Plus, Muriel had the most responsive sexuality of any person Lila had ever slept with. Lila learned from the beginning that it was by making love to someone else, feeling how sopping wet she was, feeling her quiver, feeling her nipples change, that made Muriel excited. She was so sensitive to a lover's body that the higher she took them, the higher she went herself. When Lila was almost coming, Muriel would say her name over and over again, in her own rhythm. It all felt like one person sharing, not only the orgasm, but the climb, the floating, the coming and the falling. When Muriel came, her clitoris suddenly relaxed and Lila's fingers went through, right to the bone. Then there was a whimper and then kisses, cunty, hairy kisses between two very close bodies. Then they were themselves again, immediately, as Muriel jumped up for a glass of water. When she came back, Lila was sitting on the edge of the mattress. Muriel sat beside her, with her arms around Lila, the smell of her cunt, sort of sour, waxy apricot rising around them.

"It's funny how quickly we make love."

"It's fun making love with you Lila, I know that whatever happens, it's going to feel great."

She sat on the floor and touched Lila's thighs. She parted Lila's pubic hair and teased her cunt. Lila lay back on the mattress and let Muriel bring her face between her legs, like the breeze itself, but it was a woman, not an element. Lila forgot about thinking and lived through her cunt, perceiving the world as only warm and sweet and deeply powerful.

Then, Muriel decided to wake her up and take her somewhere else, so her tongue got more circular and purposeful. Eventually, Lila knew and could anticipate that, as it came around her clit, Muriel's tongue was going to flick suddenly, in the same place. Each time she wanted that moment more and more until that flicker became the entire feeling. Lila was taken over by the beat of perfect pressure, more and more, and she was moving and talking, crying out. Muriel's face started to turn, putting her head more and more into Lila's vagina. Lila saw her jaw go up and down and heard her gasping for air, keeping the pressure, keeping her tongue round and round until Lila pushed into her face and came, and fell back down on the bed as Muriel's large body crawled over her with kisses.

By nine o'clock they were buying apricots on Second Avenue and kissing good-bye amidst the uptown intermission crowd at The Orpheum Theatre as each set off into her own Saturday night.

TWENTY

The heat finally came and with it the loss of desire to move very far or fast, as well as a certain loss of hope. Lila sat naked, writing, knowing that it was too hot for anyone to care about seeing her pounds of flesh. She had work to do and wasn't going to dissipate her time by going over to The Inn to hang out. Why go? She'd see Emily and they would be awkward with each other, then the special mood between them would be ruined. Better to just sit home. But her chest started to tighten, the typewriter keys got heavy, cigarettes made her throat sore. She was dying, dying in the heat.

Finally, seeing no other option, Lila wandered off to The Inn where everyone was hanging out in the back, drinking beer and chatting. It was someone's birthday and the theme was poolside. There were little wading pools, Hawaiian shirts and bathing suits. These girls always had cute little themes to the things they did, it was more fun that way. It was tackiness as an acquired and desired aesthetic instead of tackiness because that was the only way one knew how to be. A subtle but crucial difference.

Lila talked to Sheena for a while about Krishna, the house-painting business and good places to go bowling. Meanwhile, a film of Helen Hayes mud wrestling was being projected onto a brick wall. Lila noticed an extremely tall muscular woman in a Straight to Hell t-shirt leaning against the wall, one booted foot flat against the brick. Even more interesting was the green dragon tattoo that seemed to be winding its way down her left arm. Her blonde hair was long and shaggy and she had a black bandana tied around her pants leg. Then Lila noticed that this woman was staring right at her from across the wading pool. When she caught Lila's eye she came closer, then closer.

"I'm Nancy," she said, dangling her beer bottle from two fingers.

"Hi Nancy, I'm Lila."

"I know."

"Oh, well, why don't you pull up a chair?"

But she preferred to stand. Helen Hayes' new girlfriend was not at all what Lila had expected. She thought Helen would go for someone little and dizzy, forgetting for a moment that there is a reason why there are butches and femmes in this world. Nancy was on a serious mission to check out the competition and make sure that Helen's honor was in no way compromised.

"I read that story you gave Helen. Everything was fine except for the part where you said she was jerky-looking. I didn't like that."

"Oh, don't worry Nance, it was all in fun, you know. I was just joking around, nothing serious."

"Good, because it's real between Helen and me."

"That's wonderful, I'm very happy for you both."

Lila had the strange premonition that she was about to be challenged to a duel. But suddenly the tone changed as Nancy grabbed a chair, plopped herself down and started a very friendly conversation about, of all things, theatre.

"You know I have a very strong background in theatre and Helen, she's so modest, she needs my encouragement and guidance."

"Oh yes, Helen Hayes is modesty personified."

"I'm glad you understand." Nancy relaxed now, opening a

fresh can of beer while making a perfect shot with the old bottle into a garbage can on the other side of the party.

"Helen feels bad that she doesn't have the exposure and the experience that she needs, so this summer I'm giving her plays to read to expand her theatrical sense."

"I know, she's so shy and retiring."

"Yeah, well, it's the least I can do."

Lila watched as Nancy proceeded to open a third beer with one hand and crush the empty one with the other. *Boy,* she thought, *Helen certainly knows how to pick 'em wild and woolly.*

"So I gave her these reading assignments, some Chekhov, for the characterization, *Zoo Story* for the vernacular, *A Doll's House* for the structure, *Death of a Salesman* for the death."

"*Cat on a Hot Tin Roof* for the tin?" Lila suggested, trying to be helpful. "*Breakfast at Tiffany's* for the breakfast?"

"What?"

"Never mind." Lila decided she had better learn to control her instinct to turn every conversation into some kind of sick joke.

Over their heads, on the wall, Helen and her challenger were rolling and romping, caked in brown mud. Helen's shirt was falling off and her nipples were smeared in dirt.

"Well, Nancy, I'm really glad we had this opportunity to talk, so you can be one hundred percent sure that there are no hard feelings whatsoever. I'm sure you and Helen will be very happy."

"Ms. Subways, there you are."

Thank God, it was Isabel Schwartz to the rescue. Lila smiled good-bye to Nancy and walked over to Isabel to hear her new ideas, since she had that I-need-to-talk-to-you-right-away-because-I-have-a-new-idea expression.

"Ms. Sub-Gum Ways, I have got a great idea for the new show. It's based on your experience with Helen. I'll play you and I'll keep running into different kinds of girls who promise all sorts of undeliverable delights and in the end, I become the Messiah, or better yet, Michael Jackson. We'll ask Helen to play herself. She'll do it, don't you think? Anything for Art. Miss Subways? What's the matter? You look like you're going out of order."

"I think I'm making a series of local stops."

"Hi Lila." There was Emily who smiled as though she didn't know what else to do and so turned away abruptly with that smile still plastered on her face and then walked back into the bevy of bathing beauties frolicking by the beach umbrella.

"That girl is trouble, buddy, I'm telling you. Girls like that don't go for girls like us. We don't get girls like that."

"Miss Schwartz, why not? I mean, why not? Know what I mean?"

"You don't understand," Isabel explained carefully after securing a purple shoe lace, "First of all, she's a WASP, they don't feel emotions deeply like we do. Catholics might stab you in the back, but afterwards they're upset if you don't like them any more. Protestants don't care what you think when they're through with you. They're just used to having everything their way. Besides, she's slumming it right now. They think it's boho to hang out with all these dark people with idealistic goals, but sooner or later they get tired of buying their shoes at Fava and go into antiqueing, or something useless like that. They don't know about the kinds of things that we know about and what's more, they don't care about the kinds of things that we know about. But, I know you can't hear that now. Well, maybe you'll get some good material at least. Remember, when your heart is breaking, write it down. When a relationship is over, what do you have? You have nothing. But if you write it down, you have material. That's the best a girl can hope for in these troubled times."

"What about you Isabel, don't you ever get shot in the gut from Cupid's bow?"

"I'm not falling in love until 1990. I refuse to be romantic during the Reagan era. I'm waiting for a Democratic president."

Lila intuited that Isabel was right. She was going to let herself get totally obsessed and ultimately used as a doormat by some woman just because she had neat hair. But, for old times' sake, she had to let herself sink, once again, into the muck and mire of failed pursual. It reminded her that she was alive. So, Lila hung out and hung out and hung out and drank beers and talked to girls and waited.

Emily came up to her some hours later, smiled again and said, "I'm glad you came. So many people that I like are here tonight."

Another appropriately vague, but pleasant comment. Lila got disgusted with herself and then she got sad, pulled herself together, resigned, and put her arm around Emily's shoulder.

"Emily, I'm going home now." She kissed Emily's hair, relaxed and natural, and turned away. Lila could hear the violins on the soundtrack as she stepped outside onto the deserted street and was in the movies again, walking off into the sunrise. But, for some reason having to do with the various emotional patterns that intersect in that field called love, Emily had followed her out and leaned against the building.

There was something very beautiful to Lila about the sight of a sweating woman leaning against a building on a summer city night.

"Lila, would you like me to walk you home? I'm pretty tired, but I like being around you."

Then there was a real smile and a wriggle, the way that women tremble sometimes when they're happy and excited.

"Sure Emily, I like being with you too. I really do."

And Lila was so very deeply touched.

TWENTY-ONE

There are moments that stand out delightful and clear like a black and white photograph. The first forty times you look at it, the whole event comes to life, your life with that person, frozen, smiling in her youth on a late night street corner, and that moment becomes the whole experience until, long after you've separated and lost each other, you have only one thing left, that moment. Lila had gone over it again and again in her head.

"I'm not a cold person," Emily had said and hugged her, held her face between her hands and kissed it, held her again and clasped her hand. "I don't want you to think I'm a cold person."

When Emily had walked with her into the apartment that evening, Lila was so overcome with shyness that she had to put on her mirrored sunglasses for the first ten minutes or so, just to be able to speak. But then, they eased so gracefully into their wonderful talks, full of understanding, like a gift with all its erotic properties.

Talk in the living room, talk in the bedroom, talk up on the rooftop, watching the never-ending light patterns of the city change their shape and sequence. And all the while Lila was thinking *dolce*, wanting to touch this woman. Wishing for it on a star, on a white seagull illuminated in the moonlight, on a green caterpillar inching across the concrete.

When Emily decided to leave, they walked silently down Second Avenue until Lila felt foolish, like a shadow who knows that night is coming, and turned to go back. But, like a worried lover, like an older woman in a thirties movie touched under a streetlight by the innocence of another, thoughtful, anxious, emotional, Emily hugged her, kissed her face, put her hands on Lila's cheeks and hugged her again.

"I don't want you to think I'm a cold person," Emily said, holding her hand before turning away.

And all the way home Lila was thinking *dolce, dolce* and looked up to see Tina, tired and hot, writing in her journal in the empty gelatti store. And everything seemed possible again.

PART THREE

TWENTY-TWO

J une eighth was the first major demonstration of the summer. Old friends and neighbors greeted each other on the subways and buses as they headed towards the United Nations to protest United States intervention in Central America. In the U.S. people are allowed to be political as long as they don't actually have an effect on anything. So, the purpose of these gatherings was for the like-minded to see each other, try to get thirty seconds on the evening news and remember that they were not as alone as they felt reading the paper in the morning. Throughout, there was an unspoken hope that sooner or later someone would figure out a more effective method for accomplishing their goals.

The crowd was a fairly large one considering the one hundred degree weather. It hovered somewhere near ten thousand. The participants were mostly white, mostly from local peace groups and small political organizations. This included a lot of older people. Some were lifetime members of the Communist Party or upstarts from Another Grandmother for Peace, or both. They were joined by a small contingent of veterans of the Abraham Lincoln Brigade, fighters against facism in the Spanish Civil War. They got a big cheer from the dehydrated crowd.

This particular demonstration had been organized by Artists Against War and so, instead of long, boring, speeches, the Plaza was set up as a collection of simultaneous performance spaces from which a cacophony of overlapping productions filled the air. A Black woman rapped to a white man's saxophone while a Saint Mark's Poetry Project poet yelled his esoteric observations. Two women did an interpretive dance in very hot costumes to the synthesizer of yet another experimental band. At exactly the same moment, The New York Marxist School Chorus sang *El Pueblo Unido*. It was definitely different from the usual demo, Lila observed, but not actually better, being so chaotic and finally, meaningless.

After a few hours of disorganized mass sweating, the crowd started to march up Madison Avenue towards Reagan's reelection campaign headquarters. Having been around a bit, Lila managed to bump into a few people she saw only at protest marches. A theoretical Marxist who used to live down the hall. He had married a corporate lawyer and the two of them had just gotten back from Nicaragua. An old acquaintance from a now defunct food co-op was finishing her dissertation and had also just come back from Nicaragua.

"What are you doing these days Lila?"

"Nothing."

It was too complicated to go into.

Then she was faced with the usual dilemma of having to decide which contingent to march with. In other words, which part of her complex identity would be the base from which to express her opposition to the latest outrage? Ideally she would have loved to find a sign proclaiming "Girls Against War." However, the only banner relating in any way to anyone female came from a small left party that always had signs proclaiming "Women for Somebody Else." There was also a "Lesbians and Gays for Jesse Jackson" placard, but that seemed a little too specific, although she would definitely have carried one saying "Jesse Jackson for Lesbians and Gays." She tried the New Jewish Agenda Brooklyn Chapter, but after half a block decided, in all good conscience, she couldn't march with a group from Brooklyn. As always, she finally ended up with an ad-hoc collection of vaguely associated dykes, all without places to march.

They tried out a few creative slogans, since slogan writing is second nature to urban lesbians.

"Cruise People, Not Missiles."

"More Dykes, No Nukes."

And the old favorite:

"Two-Four-Six-Eight, Smash the Family, Smash the State."

But the t-shirted men with megaphones kept drowning them out with "No Draft, No War, US Out of El Salvador."

A noble sentiment, thought Lila, *but a very mundane delivery.*

After she got home and washed off the sweat, Lila dressed up in a red and black fifties print dress, tacky large earrings and a matching red and black imitation alligator skin clutch bag. She was off again to hang around outside of a women's dance, since it was too expensive to actually go in. She stopped off, of course, to visit Emily and invited her to come hang outside too, when that night's show was over.

Taking the circuitous route, Lila ran into Ray in his red "Enjoy Cocaine" t-shirt, cut off right above the navel so he could put his hands on his stomach muscles whenever he felt like it.

"Lila, I've been thinking it over and I figured it all out."

"What have you got figured out?"

"It has to do with those immigrants," he said, shifting his gaze now and then. "Look around at those Koreans who own all the fruit stands. They'll hire a Black man to stand outside with a stick and hit someone who tries to steal fruit. The Arabs own the delis, the Indians own the newsstands and wouldn't give credit on a pack of rolling papers. The way I see it, we, the Americans, used to be the insiders, but now we are the outsiders. Now, have you been to Harlem lately?"

"No."

"Well it's filled with everything but Black people. White people in brownstones, Orientals with those fruit stands, and when

I walk down the street they look at me weirdly, like, 'Are you a *Negro?'* Hey brother, I got good sense here."

Ray ran off to a brown Chevy to sell a bag. He was back in a flash.

"I know from the sixties," he said, scratching his grey beard and smiling with his eyes, "'cause I was around then and you were too young, but in the sixties, most people didn't understand what was happening, and I'm not talking color now either. Most people just followed the trend and said what they were supposed to say, but only a few understood the whole analysis. Fifteen years ago we turned Tompkins Square Park into a people's park. All kinds of people were sleeping there, talking about changing things and the police came to break it up. Last night just as many people slept out in that park but it was because they had no other place to go, so the police don't give a damn."

Another car drove by looking for stuff.

"Sense," Ray said, running up to the car. "I got skunk and sense."

So Lila went over to the dance and hung out on the sidewalk for a few hours, waiting for Emily to come, knowing that she would. Finally she saw her, standing off to one side, sort of alone in the crowd. Times were so bad that the sidewalk was packed and hardly anybody had paid to go inside where there was a live DJ. Someone had brought a radio and a big box and someone else had brought tapes and all the poor lesbians were dancing and chatting and having a good old time. And Lila had a good time too until it got really late and she accompanied Emily back to where she was house-sitting on Fourth Street.

TWENTY-THREE

They sat shirtless in the heat, on the fire escape watching the costume shop across the way bustle with sewing and cutting. It was the one lit unit, frantic with activity.

"Lila, would you like to sleep here tonight?"

Lila was beginning to grow accustomed to the idea that she rarely understood exactly what Emily was trying to tell her.

"I'd be real happy if you did, but I'm feeling kind of sleepy."

"Sure, hey, why not."

So, once again, Lila crawled into this woman's bed. This time though, their breasts were shiny from moonlight on sweat. Lila lay there, listening to Emily fall asleep and felt like a really stupid asshole. What was Emily trying to pull anyway? Was she totally out of it or was she purposely trying to make a fool of her? What the fuck was Lila doing in this situation? She should just get dressed and get the hell home. She heard Emily start to snore and some different levels of thought entered her mind. She really didn't want to let all this effort go out the window. Maybe Emily just wasn't meant to be her lover. Maybe Emily was her Carlo Marx or Dean Moriarty. Maybe she was someone to go out on adventures with and talk things over with all night long. Maybe Lila was being given the precious gift of a partner, a chum for adventures. Suddenly she wanted to jump up and read a chapter from *On The Road*.

"Are you anxious, Lila?"

"Me? Anxious? Of course."

"Are you changing your mind? Do you want to go home now?"

"No, Emily, I. . . look, I thought you wanted to sleep with me. That's why I came home with you. Look Emily, tell me the truth. What are you trying to pull here anyway? I mean, I don't always understand all the time what you mean by what you do."

"Why do I have to initiate everything?" Emily asked, with impatience in her voice, as though it was all so obvious.

"Oh. So that's how it is."

Lila touched Emily's hair and her face and the soft folds of her neck. At that moment, Emily moved the same way any woman moves when her aching skins finally gets touched in just the right way.

"I'm sorry I don't have a lot of energy," Emily said, reaching for her, "I'm usually too sleepy to make love late at night. I'll have to come visit you sometime during the day. Oh, I love your breasts."

And then it all began. You look at a woman and know she is a lesbian but you don't always know why until you find out one day how much she loves to suck your breasts. With bursts of hidden energy and force, Emily sucked Lila's breasts and looked up at her red nipple between her own red lips and flicked her tongue back and forth in Lila's direction. She kissed Lila so hard on the mouth that Lila could feel Emily's skull through her lips. Emily gave her her breasts to kiss, going back to Lila's breasts, to her mouth, to her breasts, her mouth, all with determination until she'd used her fingers to fuck Lila, until the whole of Emily's body was in her fingers, sweating and moving. . .

"Lila, am I hurting you?"

"What? No! You feel wonderful to me."

Lila looked closely at Emily's cunt, all sleek and symmetrical, following each fold and crease with her tongue until Emily pulled her up.

"You don't want me to come yet darlin'."

She was lying on Lila, sliding against her on a layer of sweat, putting her delicate face between Lila's legs, and when Lila came, Emily pulled herself up along her body, hanging out on her chest.

"Do you feel good darling? I want you to feel good."

Then she said, "I'm sorry I don't have much energy. Good night."

What Lila really wanted was to kiss her neck a hundred times and tell her how sweet she was and how good she'd made her feel. She wanted to whisper to Emily about how exciting it was to be held in her arms, strong from carrying boxes in the factory, in her fishnets. But instead, Lila just lay back and watched Emily sleep. Lila lay there with an enormous grin on her face.

When Emily woke up at six the next morning to go to work, Lila watched her put cocoa butter on her hairless legs and vaseline around her eyes. She watched Emily walk off with her red plastic handbag and powder blue booties. What a wonderful thing to have to dream about all the hot day long, Lila thought on her way to the office. This is what she wanted from her life. Nine o'clock on a blistering morning, riding up a stifling elevator to a stifling job thinking about Emily's fingers inside her, feeling them still. That was it.

TWENTY-FOUR

"Lila, sometimes I just need to be quiet."

It was Friday night out on the stoop and Emily didn't feel like talking. So, they watched the street a while longer until Lila got involved in a detailed conversation with an Italian Buddhist. Then they started walking slowly over to Washington Square Park, where they sat on the littered grass until it was too disgusting. They moved to some benches until men harassed them away and ended up at the midnight show of *Blade Runner* at The Saint Mark's. They walked in late and Lila couldn't figure out what was going on. Since she didn't have a TV, she found it harder and harder to tolerate movies, or even just to follow them. Her eyes hurt from too many screen flashes and all the marijuana smoke in the theatre and she didn't understand why Emily was being so stiff.

Finally they left that scene and wandered a bit, ending up on Lila's roof, lying on a blanket between the tarpaper and the open sky. Emily stayed distant and cool.

"I think touching somebody's body, well, I take it seriously, it's so personal. Sometime I get afraid of being abandoned. I like being with you Lila, like I said, but I'm not sure which way every friendship should go."

Lila watched Emily consider whether she should be her lover or not. She watched her have a thought, decide to articulate it and then do so.

"You know I'm not sexually adventurous. I'd rather not have sex and wait for something important and good for me to happen. You seem to have a lot of girfriends, or at least try to, like you're not worried about being thwarted. How do you handle sexual fantasies about so many different people at once?"

"I always need to have some image in my head. Sometimes I feel like a certain kind of sex, then I look around to see what's out there."

Listening to her own words made Lila consider that she might actually be crass, promiscuous, coarse and in every way stupid. It was just at that moment that Emily abruptly put her face to Lila's breasts and started to kiss them. She put her face into Lila's lap and caressed her bare, hairy legs. This time Lila knew that Emily's cunt lived in her breasts and she looked at them, smelled them, felt their textures dry and wet, pressed her nipples, flattened them with her tongue and forgot that a few minutes before she had felt like a complete jerk.

"I love breasts," Emily said and Lila felt so close to her that she saw a glow of flush and neon light vibrating around Emily's face, like she was enchanted or emanating power. Lila wanted to talk while they were touching, to drown Emily in mush, to tell her how beautiful it was to make love with her.

"Lila, are you falling asleep?"

"No, no sorry, I just got lost in feeling you."

"Because I want to have sex, so wake up." She laughed out loud.

"Okay," Lila said, grinning, "Let's have sex."

But first, they stopped to share a cigarette, naked on the rooftop. Sitting together, they both reached over and felt each other's wetness while Emily smoked. Lila sat behind her, easing her into her arms, holding Emily's head on her breasts.

While they watched the night lights of the city, the red, white and blue Empire State Building, Lila reached down into Emily's cunt.

"Have you every been touched like this before, while you were smoking a cigarette?" she asked.

"No. Why?"

"Because of the suspense," Lila said and stroked Emily's clitoris around and around while the ash burned. As the smoke went up in a straight line into the sky, Lila held Emily's breast, feeling each duct of her large red nipple. Emily smiled holding that glowing cigarette, moved and quietly came, curling up relaxed and natural.

Later, after different kinds of sex and feelings, Emily was so soft that Lila kept thinking as she watched her, *I want to be close to this woman.*

Morning on the roof began at five-thirty when the sun suddenly and brutally came pounding down over the still-tired refugees from hot crowded apartments, starting the day off grimy and stale. They woke up and Emily's affection was gone again. Lila could have taken a shower and sucked Emily's breasts all morning but Emily went off to do something, leaving Lila sitting there sweating on the roof, watching the city get ready for another sweltering day.

TWENTY-FIVE

Coney Island still looked the way it had always looked. There were crowds of poor people in tacky clothing, thousands of screaming children and an amusement park becoming more and more fantasy-provoking in its imposing decline. Only, when Emily and Lila walked the boardwalk that Sunday afternoon, the poor people were Caribbean and Greek and Russian and East Asian and Hispanic. They sold *cerveza fría* and cooked crabs, freshly caught off the pier from the filthy ocean water.

Lila had finally found a lover who could out-distance her. A lifetime of playing it cool had not prepared her for the on-again off-again affections of Emily Harrison. Lila didn't like couples and she didn't want to know what her girlfriends were doing all the time, but, when she was hanging around with someone, she liked for them to be emotionally present. That didn't seem unreasonable. She liked to touch and kiss and play and say how much she liked being with them and how wonderful it had been the night before when that someone made love to her with her mouth, asking first,

"Lila, do you mind if I eat you out?"

Emily, however, who had spent her life moving in and out of

intimacy, was, by habit or caution, on the reserved side. Lila, feeling stymied, stared out at the Atlantic Ocean, picturing herself turning to mush, a nerd, a namby-pamby, a pansy.

When they got off the F train back from the beach, Emily asked,

"Do you want to come over?"

"Yeah," Lila answered, not quite sure of what she was expected to say. "I mean, as long as you don't think we've been spending too much time together or anything."

"Listen Lila, if you're going to sleep with me, you have to be my friend," Emily responded, appearing taller than Lila had ever noticed before, "You have to come and go as you please. You have to be a little more butch and not keep asking me if I want to be with you or not."

Lila swallowed her pride and went over to Emily's, took a shower and fell asleep naked on the bed while Emily sat on the floor sewing one of her creations. Hours later, waking up from a sleep, deep only as an escape from embarrassment, Lila felt Emily come sit by her feet. By this time, Lila knew enough to understand that Emily was not going to lie down beside her, put her delicious arms around her and whisper all the ways that she was going to make love to her. So, Lila took off Emily's clothes and they licked each other's vaginas, more for the fact of doing it than for a sexual feeling. Lila took Emily in her arms, and made love to her in a close, old-fashioned way.

"Lila, I'm worried that I'm not giving you an orgasm."

Lila found both the content and timing of this statement slightly surprising but she had already noticed that she and Emily saw identical situations with completely different eyes.

"I've been celibate for so long Lila, I'm not used to making love. When I think about this, about being with you, I think it's a good thing. We have a good sexual relationship, but I don't feel at all sentimental about it. This is something fun we can do together, but it has to keep that cutting edge of hostility so that it doesn't get boring."

"Sure," Lila said, thinking that if she tried to understand

totally Emily's rapidly changing moods and perceptions, she wasn't going to make any progress at all. "Now, how do you feel about having your asshole touched?"

"What do you mean? Putting your fingers in it? No, that sounds painful."

"I was thinking more about licking and sucking."

"That sounds alright," Emily said, "but not anything in it. Since I was raped, I can't stand anything inside me at all.''

There was sand all over the bed.

"Sometimes Lila, I can't stand for certain people to even touch my breasts. What about you? What do you like?"

"Oh, everything. I don't care. Whatever you want to do is fine with me."

At this Emily laughed and laughed, pushing down on Lila's cunt just to check her out clinically. Then she made love to Lila, who helped, telling her where to put her hands and when and how fast, like they were making love to Lila together.

"You know Emily, I don't expect you to be the greatest lover I ever had. Just do what you want. Sometimes I make love to you with my mouth for you, and sometimes it's for me. I just feel a need for that shot of saltiness on my tongue. I don't care if it's not always the precisely correct motion. I like it when you move around. It makes me wonder what you're going to do next and I get turned on by thinking that that's what you want to do."

Since, by that time, it was late Sunday night and Emily had to be up by six to go to the factory the next day and then had to sew costumes for the Inn's new show all the next evening, they walked to the corner of Saint Mark's Place.

"Good-bye," Emily kissed her. "Come see me."

She kissed Lila again, smiling. "Call me even if you just want to talk." They kissed, surrounded by the late weekend throng. "Really darlin', don't lose touch with me." They kissed, they kissed and parted.

"You should be ashamed of yourself," Lila heard a male voice sputter from the crowd as she ran towards her home.

TWENTY-SIX

The office was so hot, Lila's sweat was dripping into the new electronic typewriter and she was afraid she would electrocute herself. Fed up with the glare of fluorescent lights, Vicki, the office manager, suggested they go out on the PATH train to her mother's house, pick up the car and some plants and drive back to the city. Vicki and her five-year girlfriend Beverly had recently moved from Jersey to Harlem as a way of being in Manhattan and still being around Black people.

Lila and Vicki's friendship had gone down some rocky paths. Like when Vicki got political and Lila tried to get political. They would sit and rap and think about everything in a new way. Sometimes it felt to Lila that she was on the border of earth-shattering revelations. Other times she wondered if this wasn't just another in a life-long series of mind-fucks.

"Have you ever made love with a woman of color?" Vicki asked.

"Well, no."

"That's what I mean," Vicki had said, disgustedly lighting another cigarette. "You white women who claim to support our movement, but you won't let a woman of color into your bed."

Lila didn't quite know what to think. Maybe Vicki had a

point. Why hadn't she ever come on to a woman of color? Of course, no woman of color had ever come on to her either. But then again, so fucking what? That wouldn't prove anything. Men slept with women all the time and they still didn't understand them.

Then Vicki became a macrobiotic. "Macroneurotic" Lila called it. Lila could just sit for hours watching Vicki eat her concoctions out of little plastic containers during lunch. She always ate a lot and fast as if it was the most delicious thing she had ever tasted.

"What's that Vick?"

"Want some?"

"What is it?"

"Miso-tahini spread on rice cakes."

"Oh." Lila could never get used to the fact that those rice cakes were really food. They tasted like a mixture of styrofoam and nothing.

But Vicki got awfully healthy looking, she lost a lot of weight and stopped smoking and stopped drinking and stopped eating dairy, meat, sugar, wheat and eggs.

"Lila," she moaned one afternoon, "I'm bored. I want a corned beef sandwich," and another chapter was over.

Lately Vicki had been trying to figure how to get out of her relationship with Beverly, which meant that she **and Lila could** drop the discourse for a while and just hang out, talking about women.

"The other day, my brother came over," Vicki said, "and I told him Beverly and I weren't getting along. He asked me if I was worried that she was going to leave me and I said, *Shit no, I'm worried that she'll never leave me*. I asked her to move out and the next thing she did was put in shelves. She doesn't want to go."

"Poor you," Lila said, teasingly. "You've got what most people in the world spend their whole lives trying to find, a devoted lover who will stay with you always. Life's tough."

"That's easy for you to say, Lila Futuransky," answered

Vicki, smiling and playing with her dreds, "'cause you're not hooked. Wait till that Emily girl gets a grip on you, it'll all be over so fast, you won't know what hit you."

They walked outside to the store to get some Doritos and two Cokes, past all the well-kept lawns and new cars lining the affluent Black neighborhood.

"Everyday I see a woman who's, well you know, sexy, fine legs or such, and I'd rather sit alone in a room and think about them than be eaten out by Beverly in a black bodice and whip. Maybe she'll get a girlfriend, I keep hoping. I tell her to go out with other people and if I hear that someone has a crush on her I invite them over for dinner. Oh Jesus."

They got in Vicki's car and started the drive past Elizabeth and Newark back to the city. They sang along with the radio for a while, but they didn't know any of the same songs so then they started talking about their grandmothers. Vicki's had worked the land in Louisiana, Lila's worked the land in Lithuania. Both of their moms used to take them to the library to read books. Both of their moms freaked out when they got new ideas from the books they read. Both had inherited remnants of poverty that they were the first generation to avoid.

"You know, one thing I retain from my grandmother," Vicki said, "is her thing about aluminum foil. I can afford aluminum foil, but just like when she came up to live with us in Jersey, I still save every teeny-tiny scrap and stick it in my drawer."

"It's wild how that stuff stays with you," Lila agreed. "My one grandmother was a peasant in Russia, destitution level. But life is so strange, one day she was eating potatoes in the Motherland and fifty years later she was watching color TV in New Jersey. But even when she had some bucks, she still added rice to stretch her chopped meat. My other grandmother was from Austria where things were alright for Jews. Her family was doing okay and had pretty high expectations. After the First World War they lost it all, had to come here and she worked in a laundry in Brooklyn for the rest of her life. But you know, that woman always had cream in her coffee."

At that moment two Van Halen fans drove by in a dirty white Chevy. One leaned out the window in Lila and Vicki's direction and shouted,

"Suck my cock you Black bitch."

They sat in silence for a minute.

"You take one step into America and look what happens," Vicki said, and then hummed to herself. "At least that's one way of looking at it." She snapped on the radio again and they listened to the interference as they drove through the Holland Tunnel. But by the time the car came up at Canal Street the incident was filed away along with the others and they were chattering like normal again. Scores of Chinese boys were waving at the cars, selling firecrackers for the Fourth of July. They were hawking and smoking, trying to look tough, like Rocky, with rolled up t-shirt sleeves holding hard packs of Marlboros, puffing out their chests.

"Oh no," Vicki said, "I hate the Fourth of July. Between the bombs and the flags, it's too American for me. Even uptown it sounds like a war is going on. I'm going camping this year, to get away from that red, blue and *white*."

Vicki dropped Lila off on Third Avenue instead of taking her to her door because Lila just needed to take a look at everything again. She passed the Polish butcher and the Korean fruit stands and the Chinese take-out and the Arab deli and the Greek coffee shop and the East Asian newsstand and the Jewish bakery. She realized that she had been getting lost in the world of romance and hadn't been looking at things as closely as she usually did. She'd been preoccupied with love and missed out on enjoying the beauty of the Lower Eastside everyday. Plus, she hadn't been thinking about Jack or tripping the streets or imagining adventures. It was like waking up when you've slept all day and you know it's night, but you don't know which one.

Then she remembered to run upstairs and turn on the radio right away because Lacy was being interviewed at that very moment.

"I'd like to welcome our listening audience to another episode of *Write-On America*, a program funded by the National Endowment for the Arts. Today we are pleased to have as our guest, Miss Lacy Burns, a Black woman poet who many people believe, and I agree, is destined to be the next Lorraine Hansberry. Tell us Miss Burns, you have a young son, am I right?"

"Yes, Kwame, and he's listening right now. Can I say hello? Hello, Kwame."

"Charming. And, how do you, a single mother, find time to hold down a job, raise a son and write poetry?"

"I am not a single mother. I have a husband. His name is Arthur. He's a painter."

"Oh I see. I'm sorry, that's what's written on this paper. There must have been a mistake in the research department. Anyway, let us move on to the next question. I assume that you have been heavily influenced by Nikki Giovanni."

"No, not really."

"I ask you that because I would like for you to talk to our audience about how you view poetry as a tool for social change."

"I don't know really. I don't know how many people read poetry and those who do. . . well. . . I don't know how many of them will be motivated to social action from reading about my son or my garden."

"Oh I see. Well, Miss Burns, that's very interesting. May I call you Lacy?"

"Why not?"

"Lacy, I enjoyed your first book a great deal and I'm excited to hear that your new one will be out this fall. The aspect of your work that I find the most inspiring is the brilliant way in which you capture the vernacular. How long did it take you to develop a voice rich with the natural rhythms of the streets?"

"Actually, that's just the way me and my friends talk."

Lila turned off the radio and poured herself a glass of milk. Everyone she knew or encountered had their own particular reality but what they all shared was a common difficulty with keeping to it in the face of mounting adversity.

TWENTY-SEVEN

There was Solomon on the stoop deep in conversation with a tall Black man in a Malcolm X t-shirt. "By Any Means Necessary" was printed across his chest.

"Hey Solomon," Lila called out.

"Lila, Lila, I am glad to see you. This is my friend Jonathan. Tell her what you just told me Johnny. This is Lila. Tell her."

Solomon took out a Players and put on a serious expression.

"There were about ten fellows come by to look at your building today. You better watch out. That landlord of yours is trying to sell it. He's asking seven hundred thousand dollars."

"For this piece of shit? He only paid sixty thousand two years ago. The speculation going on around here is unreal. There's mice, roaches, a leaky roof, the windows don't fit the frame so the wind blows through, the floorboards are coming up in spots."

"You know it, you know it." Solomon shook his head.

"You had better watch out. The new landlord's gonna want to double your rent roll right away, just to start to cover costs. You know Mister Pilinero, the old Italian in apartment four?"

"Yeah?"

"The old guy got pneumonia and went into the hospital last

week. This morning his apartment was advertised for rent in the paper for twelve hundred dollars a month and the man ain't even dead yet."

"Twelve hundred dollars! I earn half of that in a month."

"Well, you'd better watch your ass Lila. They gonna be turning off the heat, robbing your apartment, refusing to make repairs."

"Twelve hundred dollars," she repeated, "I can't get over it. What kind of rich person would want to spend twelve hundred dollars a month to live here, with us?"

"There ain't gonna be no *us* by the time they move in. That's where the master plan comes in." Jonathan was pleased because now he had an opening where he could launch into his *master plan* theory.

"This is landlord city, Lila, landlord city." Solomon was rocking back and forth, drawing deeply and pensively on his cigarette.

Lila's landlord was a notorious scum. A Hassid from Brooklyn, he claimed that the tenants had formed an association because they were anti-Semitic.

"Your building is owned by a rich synagogue," Jonathan said. "There's five millionaire rabbis and they own practically the whole block."

"Hey Jonathan, let's not get carried away with Jewish conspiracy theories please, because I really want to like you. Let's just say it's one lone snake."

"Five rabbis, I tell you, and they're all millionaires, every last one. Yep, you'd better watch your ass."

"This is landlord city," Solomon said again, his stetson pulled low over his forehead. "One hundred and fifty percent landlord city."

As soon as Lila got upstairs the phone rang. It was Isabel Schwartz calling from a pay phone.

"Ms. Subways, what are you doing this very minute? We've got to go over to the 8BC Club right away to see Jeff Weiss and Dorothy Cantwell. Come on buddy, two people who are actually good artists. Let's go."

So, Lila jumped. First there was 8BC and then there was Jeff Weiss, two mutually exclusive commodities co-existing in the same category of East Village theatre. The club was a renovated farmhouse on one of the most decimated blocks in New York City, Eighth Street between Avenues B and C. In fact, it was essentially one of the only living structures on the entire street, smack in the middle of a lot of smack. But, once through the unmarked doors, it was packed with young punkettes, NYU students and bisexuals, all who had descended on the defenseless neighborhood.

As for Jeff Weiss, he was another story altogether. The man was known as "the world's greatest actor" and if there was such a person it probably was him, plus he had a mythology to prove it. He did shows. He didn't care about reviews. He didn't care about grants. He barely cared if he had an audience. When you got a chance to see him in action, there might be five other people in the theatre because of his refusal to advertise, but one of them might be Susan Sontag or Meredith Monk, someone who thinks they know what's good. Or so the rumors went. Only a few people really understood the mastery of this crazy, aging writer, director and actor. His inspiration was as carefully sculpted as his pectorals, the latter the result of years of supporting himself at construction or working out on a Nautilus, whichever image appealed to your imagination. Those stories made the myth and the myth made the man. Jeff Weiss won an Obie, the off Broadway version of an Oscar, but he gave it back, and then he won it again, and gave that one back too. He was asked to sit on the board of a powerful grant-giving organization, but he refused.

"I wouldn't take your money and I certainly won't give it away."

What's more, he was good. Isabel and Lila were in ecstasy. Plus, for the same admission price they got Dorothy Cantwell, the woman who could play any part that Jessica Lange or Sissy Spacek got. A world-class actress. Another underground hero, custom-made for the give-it-all approach of Jeff Weiss.

Isabel and Lila slapped down their five dollars, and put in seventy-five cents each to split a beer, waiting for the scene to begin. First, though, Jeff had to step out into the empty club, and vigorously shake hands with Lila, Isabel and the three other people there that night. His words were so sincere.

"It's great to see you, really great to see you."

But his expression looked right through them as though he was talking to a mirror. That's because he was in fantasy land and he would bring them there too, soon enough. But first the flashlights. Everyone got one, to provide the lighting and then he shouted "One, Two, Three, Go" and they went.

In the first scene of the show Jeff did a moment between two men having sex with each other at The Saint Mark's Bath. He played both parts to perfection. The second scene was called "Connie Visits His Sister In A Psychiatric Hospital Two Days Before Her Suicide On Christmas." There was no introduction. Jeff yelled out "One, Two, Three" again and suddenly he and Dorothy took everyone to that place with all its futility and starkness. For the next seven minutes, the audience was absorbed and transported until, "One, Two, Three," it was the next scene. This time Jeff's character visited his best friend Izzy, the lesbian, played by Dorothy, who was drunk and lonely because she hadn't had a woman all winter. In eleven short minutes, the audience believed and understood Izzy's hunger, and the tender and reserved friendship between the two. And so the show went on.

Lila and Isabel were sure that they had just seen a masterful moment of human creativity. The three other people in the place agreed.

Walking home through Tompkins Square Park in the mud, Isabel had something on her mind.

"Tell me Miss Subways, is it possible to do the work for what it is, ignore the Arts Mafia, the critics and the scene and the grants, and still retain your social sanity, without having to be an outcast too?"

"Somehow, I don't think so. I can't articulate why. I just have this sense that something about doing the work makes a person lose their mind. Normal people can't live without approval for so long. What I can't figure out is whether that's a benefit or a disadvantage."

"That reminds me," Isabel said, "I think I'm getting fired from Burger Heaven, so I'm on the look-out for a new waitressing job. Let me know if you hear of anything. I tried some of those new places in the neighborhood like The Art Cafe and The Zen Cafe you know, those up-scale quiche spas with their endives. They'll never hire me. All the waitresses are punky or New Wave or Old Wave, or whatever wave is coming in at high tide, if you catch my drift. In other words, you have to be in style to be in servitude and let's face it, I'm out. I think I could end up with an attitude like Jeff Weiss, but am I talented enough to justify it?"

They walked on a few more blocks, Lila remembering that look in Dorothy Cantwell's eyes. At any given moment during the performance, the audience could look into her eyes and know that she believed everything that she was saying. It was reassuring somehow, to see true sincerity once in your life, even if it was on stage. *I wonder if we really have visions,* Lila thought, *or just a lot of energy.*

She was too inspired to go home now, so leaving Isabel at the edge of the neighborhood, Lila crossed Fourteenth Street and walked up to Kitty's girlfriend's apartment on Central Park South, just to take a peek at how the other one percent lives. Kitty would be good for a discussion on this topic. The girl had gone from rags to riches and would probably be back in rags before Labor Day. She'd gone uptown for a woman and was on her way back for the theatre and the girls, girls who were usually broke.

The apartment looked out over the park. When Lila walked into Kitty's lobby, the doorman stopped her immediately. First he made a phone call. Then he handed her a little slip of paper and punched for the elevator, which contained yet another little man. He pushed the button and accompanied Lila to Kitty's floor. He waited, watching suspiciously as she walked down the hallway, which was decorated in a late-Marriott hotel motif. Kitty greeted her at the door of her pad.

The place wasn't very large, but it had everything. Her girlfriend had a computer and a xerox machine and a cable TV hook-up with HBO in color and a stereo, Beta-Max and central air-conditioning.

"What does your girlfriend do again?"

"She's in the Mob. She has legitimate holdings like stocks and interests and various businesses and real estate, and then she has back room gambling and high interest loans. All I own are my clothes."

They looked out the window. Hansom cabs were waiting for rich tourists to step out of The Plaza for a late evening buggy ride.

"There's some government guy who lives next door," Kitty said. "Whenever he has dinner parties, the secret service closes off the whole block. I think he runs the UN or something like that."

By her own definition Kitty was married. She married for love, but into money and attributed the looming divorce to the mysterious ways of the rich.

"It's a different kind of butch/femme than we know about downtown," she confided to Lila, "where people change their mind every week about which one they are. Up here the butches sit around the table and make business deals while the femmes sit next to them. Sometimes I feel like jumping up on the table and screaming I WANT. But, I don't know what it is I want."

They stared at a silent Willie Nelson on the HBO, his face turning lavender. At the same time Marvin Gaye's last record spun on the stereo. When people accumulate a lot of gadgets, Lila noted, they like to keep them all on at the same time, just to glance at once in a while.

"You know I come from a real small town upstate. Two of

my sisters have never even been to the city. My dad worked at the state prison and sent five kids to Catholic school on an annual salary of seventeen thousand dollars. No one is supposed to even think of leaving home unless it's to get married. My mother came down here once, on the bus, just to see this place. She sniffed around, touching everything, wouldn't sit down. She couldn't figure out if I was a high-class prostitute or had just made a good match."

Kitty was a little better dressed than Lila remembered. She had on make-up and a few more grey hairs.

"Maybe I should just come back home to the East Village and pick up where I left off. I could get a job hanging lights for twenty dollars a day and handing out circulars or something."

"Kitty, it's not as easy as you think. The neighborhood has changed. The apartment situation is wildly out of control."

"I don't need an apartment. All I've got are my clothes. There's always someplace to stay."

"I don't know," said Lila, looking at the marble bathroom and the Cuisinart. "No moving around like the old days. New York is closed. Pretty soon it's just going to be bag ladies and rich people stepping over them, plus a few old timers hiding out in their rent-controlled apartments hoping no one's gonna notice. For everybody else, the city is closed."

They were quiet for a minute, not knowing where to look, till they both sat down at the same time and started staring at Willie Nelson, moving his lips.

TWENTY-EIGHT

G ay Pride Week was ushered in one rainy Sunday afternoon outside a bagel restaurant on Christopher Street.
Emily and Lila sat there eating when sounds of sweet voices,
three part harmonies carrying light church tunes, floated in off
the street. Outside a group of happy young people were clap-
ping hands in the rain, singing. They linked dripping wet arms
to sway in unison to the verses of *I Believe In Him, Praise The
Lord* and the ever popular *Amen*. It was the gay Christians from
the Metropolitan Community Church holding a gay fellowship
meeting to celebrate Gay Holy Week on Sheridan Square, right
in front of the spot where Emily and Lila were eating cinnamon
raisin bagels with scallion cream cheese.

Lila was staring very intently at Emily's face. She'd been doing that more and more lately, just looking at her. Sometimes
Lila could see it made Emily so shy she would literally sweat,
fanning herself with a paper plate like a Southern belle, like
Blanche Dubois recovering her composure. Lila found Emily
exquisitely beautiful. Not with the kind of glamour that made
men gasp when Marlene Dietrich entered the room, but a more
demure, quiet attractiveness that you had to take your time to
see. She reached out to brush Emily's hair away from her fore-

head, touching it to make sure she was really there and once again Lila's gaze came to rest on the thin, deliberate scar just above Emily's hairline. Yes, that certainly was a mystery.

"Emily, I know I asked you this a few times before but I don't remember if you answered me or not. Where did that scar come from?"

"I don't know. It happened when I was very little."

"Didn't you ever ask your mom?"

"I think I asked her once. She didn't remember either."

"Your own mother didn't remember how you got a four-inch slice across your scalp? I find that hard to believe. Maybe she did it."

"Could be."

"But Emily, aren't you even the least bit interested? This could hold the key to some long repressed childhood trauma, unleashing waves of insight."

"I already have enough traumas to think about. Let's discuss the movie."

They had just seen *A Streetcar Named Desire*. There was Vivien Leigh as Blanche, with her old-fashioned master acting style, and Marlon Brando being something exciting that wasn't exactly Stanley Kowalski. They watched this movie and both agreed that the message was too sad. It said that life is a trap and anyone who tries to create their own magic will be destroyed. That wasn't Lila and Emily's message. Or, take Stanley. A guy who gives something sweet in bed and brutalizes all the rest of the day is supposed to be romantic. That wasn't Lila and Emily's message either. They knew they couldn't create three characters like Blanche and Stella and Stan, but they knew something Tennessee Williams forgot. Even when life is sad, people still have a good time. That's what these women and all their friends were trying to say everyday, in their different ways.

Emily and Lila were both inspired by their growing communication with each other, which had to do karmicly, Lila was convinced, with Gay Pride Week, a special and rare joy surpassing any other holiday including birthdays. Each year's festivities had their own special character since gay people as a group change very quickly and things become dated, then nostalgic, then historic, in a matter of months.

As Helen Hayes had put it,

"Today's kitsch is tomorrow's collectible."

Lila's first step into mass pride was a festival in Washington Square Park sometime in the late seventies. It was a hard time for Lila, working nights at the Baskin Robbins on Seventh Avenue South, across the street from a Puerto Rican gay juice bar. The guys used to come in really stoned at three in the morning and order pineapple sundaes with peanut butter ice cream and extra marshmallow sauce. Lila was eating ice cream for three meals a day, trying to survive on $2.75 an hour. So, when Bette Midler, fresh from The Continental Baths, stepped out on that stage and sang *You've Gotta Have Friends*, Lila's gay heart just melted. *Wow, somebody wants to be our friend*. Then the drag queens came on stage for their moment in the daylight. Drag queens are the barometer of gay time, meaning different things in different sociological moments, but persisting, nevertheless. At some point, early in the gay movement, they meant freedom. Faggots knew how important it was for a man to be able to walk down the street wearing a dress and tried to articulate this to the rest of the world. By the end of the decade, however, it took on other meanings. The original movement dykes were in serious negotiations with the boys and didn't take kindly to cocksuckers getting laughs by pretending to be women. Especially when their "women" were siliconed versions of every straight man's fantasy feline. A few women, in the stylish butch look of the moment, jumped on the stage and took over the microphone, in the stylish butch move of the moment, and announced "No more. From now on, this is *Lesbian* and Gay Pride Day."

The next march that Lila attended went off smoothly enough as everyone walked, sang, cheered and smiled in the hot sun up Fifth Avenue. When they got to Central Park, however, there were women telling women to turn right for the women-only rally, and men telling men to turn left to see Patti Smith and Lou Reed. Lila turned left. Patti was great.

As in every other aspect of life, the eighties had brought the doldrums to gay pride. Things had gotten frighteningly mellow. Instead of starting off the march with Salsa-Soul Sisters Third World Women Incorporated, the onlookers were greeted by the Gay Community Marching Band, in their maroon uniforms, John Philip Sousa tunes and American flags. Instead of queens, there was the Greater Gotham Business Council. Old timers hung on though, waiting for the tide to turn back again so swish wouldn't be so embarrassing. Like Rollerina, for example, a real trooper. He was a six-foot-tall queen in a prom dress, sparkle glasses, roller skates and a magic wand, blessing every contingent.

Eating her bagel, staring at Emily, Lila was convinced somehow that the old feeling of joy would come back in 1984. There was a need around town for lots of love and silly tenderness. Ronald Reagan and the AIDS crisis had sobered up people to the fact that the long haul was far from over. Even though each person had their own personal concept of what needed to be hauled and where to.

Isabel Schwartz had the idea to change the name to Lesbian Shame Week with thousands of dykes crawling down Fifth Avenue. She was even proposing "Lesbian Shame Awards."

"It's a new concept in anti-trend t-shirts," she said.

"Anti-trend t-shirts" were Isabel's code words for things that were fashionable because they were horribly ugly or in extremely bad taste.

So, Lila sat finishing her bagel thinking about all these crazy images and how they came together into one real thing that actually made sense, which was their community, and realized the nuances were only identifiable from the inside out. Still, she was inspired and looked Emily right in the eye, smiling.

"You know," she said, after all those thoughts, "I think something sweet is in the air."

TWENTY-NINE

Lila Futuransky's key to relationships had always been knowing how to properly exert restraint. She was considering this question on the way home from having spent three great days with someone she was just beginning to love and feel close to. According to her theory, the natural response on the fourth day was to want to see them again, immediately. This impulse, she always resisted. Lila was a firm believer that it was important to hold out until the fifth day, just to make sure it wasn't filled with leftover expectations from the fourth one. The sixth day was just right for some pleasant contact like a note or brief lunch visit. Just to let them know that they were still on your mind. That way things stayed pleasant, unpredictable and most of all, without desperation. But, that Emily tricked Lila by calling her on the Monday after the Sunday and saying that she wanted to see her simply because she wanted to.

Lila sat down on the stoop of the La Mama Annex on Fourth Street across from where Emily was house-sitting. She had a packet of Drum tobacco and a jar of grapefruit juice to pass the time until Emily came home from work. She watched the evening promenade of lovers strolling together, comforting each other, holding hands without talking, or deep in talk. It was pleasant to sit under Emily's window on a warm night thinking about her.

That girl was such a femme, she always wore her purse on the same shoulder. Once, Lila took her left arm by mistake and Emily asked her to stand on the other side.

"That's a femme," Lila said. "Never move the purse, just move the girl."

Then Lila giggled, thinking that Emily would love hearing something like that said about herself, giving her a place in all the sexuality of this world. But instead, Emily pushed her face into a pout, like a silly girl hurt by a silly thing.

"Don't be angry at me baby," she said quietly. "I love you so much."

"I'm not angry at you Emily."

"I know Lila, it's just that I've had this fantasy for such a long time that one day I would have a girlfriend who loved me very deeply and one day we would be having a petty disagreement and I would say *Don't be angry with me baby, I love you so much.* And now it's come true. I'm so happy."

And her face became one huge smile. Lila saw that expression again when Emily came home that night and found Lila sitting on the steps waiting for her. They sat there together laughing, entertaining each other, watching a Puerto Rican storekeeper and his wife dance outside their bodega across the street. They talked and touched each other's faces. Lila kissed Emily's forehead and they leaned back against the building to soak in the beauty on the street.

"Emily, when you were a kid, what did you want to be when you grew up?"

"A theatre designer or a fashion designer."

"I'm very impressed, Emily. I wanted to be a stewardess."

When Lila thought about Emily as a child, she saw her on a lifetime path of visual problems, spatial concerns, angles, shapes and color matching. Her descriptions were rarely anecdotal or populated. She had almost no stories about people. Instead she talked about the way the light was in the morning, the sound of the sea, or how her own body smelled in one place as opposed to another. They climbed the dirty stairs past the "Junkies Keep Out" sign and sat on the fire escape with the radio playing in the background.

"It's pretty strange spending so much time at the Inn when I'm designing or making things. It's usually late at night and people who can't sleep or don't know what to do with themselves stop by just to talk. Sometimes I feel too busy and sometimes I'm terribly shy. You talk to people all the time too, Lila. How do you deal with it?"

"I just tell them my most intimate thoughts."

"And they never bother you again."

"Right."

They felt like making love, but Emily wanted to wash her body first.

"I need to be clean for my girlfriend."

Lila sat on the edge of the tub watching Emily in the shower. She scrubbed her nails, getting out all the ink and paint from work. She shaved under her arms and carefully cleaned her asshole and vagina. She powdered and perfumed herself while Lila thought to herself that scents last as long as memory.

"What's the matter, don't you want to bring all the muck and mire of your existence into my body?"

"Oh Lila, I didn't know you were such an earth mother."

They both laughed loudly at that one, as Emily dried herself off, and then, on impulse, she pulled Lila's shirt right off her shoulder.

"I needed to taste your nipples right away," she said. And then she sat back for a while as Lila tasted hers.

"You get so much pleasure from your breasts Emily, it's beautiful to me."

"That's why sometimes I can't stand to be touched there, by certain people I mean."

"It's too close."

"Yes, that's it."

Lila leaned over and knew, for that moment, they were that close. Lightly, sexily with care and tenderness, they made love with each other. Emily was becoming a better and more confident lover. She would come up from Lila's orgasms smiling because she knew exactly what she had given her. Emily would purr and stretch, showing off like a proud, sleek cat.

The next morning, they left the house at half past six. On the way to Emily's factory, in a moment of silence, Emily grabbed Lila's hand. The city was already starting to broil and the two women's faces were damp from sweat. Emily stopped walking, right in front of the construction site where new condominiums were going up on the corner. She turned to Lila and said,

"You can sleep with me whenever you want to. We'll try it. Come over whenever you feel like it."

And Lila was changed.

PART FOUR

PART FOUR

THIRTY

Once again Lila cut out of work early. She knew that by virtue of her own misbehavior this period of employment would soon be terminated, but she didn't give a shit. By the age of eighteen she'd already been through thirty-three different jobs. Most of them had gotten boring by the second day.

"If you liked school, you'll love work," said a poster on her refrigerator. And one on her wall said, "Work: A prison of measured time." So, knowing it was a corrupt institution, she never felt guilty about sabotaging it in little ways. Like pouring powdered sugar into word processors, or misfiling information on people who owed money for things they shouldn't have to pay for in the first place, like rent. She even heard about a programmer who programmed a computer to pay out dividends to all the programmers, but that was too high-tech for Lila's personal taste.

She sat on a bench in Washington Square Park smoking a cigarette and enjoying the bright afternoon. Two men walked by. One was sort of Italian looking, beefy, in a polyester double-knit, a gold chain and a rhinestone stud in his ear. The other was a skinny, tired drug dealer.

"Just sit here a second man, I'll be right back," the dealer said as he ran off to negotiate with an equally skinny, tired guy sporting an AC/DC tattoo.

"You making a drug deal?" Lila asked because she felt like making conversation.

"Yep. Hey babe, lemme get one of your cigarettes."

"Sure."

They sat and talked about how nice the weather was and how much easier it was to buy a nickel bag in the East Village than the West Village, because of all the undercover narcs.

"You know," Lila said, "I don't mean to deal in ethnic stereotypes or anything, but you look kind of like a cop yourself. Like, you're too healthy or something. I don't know why I said that. Maybe it's the earring."

"Why don't you tell him that," the guy said, good-naturedly pointing to the dealer. "He'd probably drop dead."

"No, I'm sure he knows better than me."

There was too much going on at the same time in that park to process it all. Junkies were dying, kids were racing skateboards up and down artificial lumps, called hills, chess players wildly hit clocks in games where speed was everything. She started to think about whether or not she had a roach buried at the bottom of her pocket that maybe she could light and get just a little high with this friendly guy. He probably had great stories. But, by that time, the dealer had returned, having made all the arrangements and Mister Polyester split without even saying goodbye. Lila finished her cigarette, watched the chess players and was on her way out when she realized that the skinny dealer and the guy with the tattoo were being led away in handcuffs by two additional undercover cops who had been posing as gay men cruising.

Lila stared, open-mouthed, at the guy who had smoked her cigarette. Her skin turned so cold she forgot who she was.

"You were right," he said, grinning ear to earring, and walked off towards Bleeker Street, satisfied at having done his duty once again. Lila, on the other hand, had come too close to something completely unnecessary and so headed straight for the nearest bar for a shot of anything.

It was a lonely bar that afternoon. One of the few remaining places on Bleeker Street where a regular person could afford to get drunk. The only other customer was Roberta, Muriel's girlfriend, in her usual forest green robes, moping under the color TV.

Lila just walked over and sat down very quietly. There was a silence of pure understanding between the two women, balancing on bar stools. Lila told the whole story from beginning to end. Roberta didn't even ask one question.

"Cops," Roberta agreed, when Lila was through, "they'll never learn how to dress."

It started to get late after a while and the dreamy staleness of an old bar in the afternoon drifted away. By the time Lila got home, she remembered that she had a date that evening with Muriel, who had decided that they just had to go out with a gang of ex-patriate bourgeois Italians. She was being dragged along with them to a performance by someone from *Roma*, all because Tina was running the light board and had promised all her friends free tickets. Lila had to admit it was kind of nice to sit in a dark theatre surrounded by beautiful olive-skinned people with large blue or black eyes, rolling their tongues. Those Italians lean all over you, Lila noted. They touch you when they talk.

"Tina's so romantic," Muriel giggled in Lila's ear. "We were lying on the grass in Washington Square Park this afternoon making out, and she started to say *I will take you to the sands of Italy. I will make a bed of sand and make love to you by the waves at night.* Too much, no?"

"So that's why Roberta was in a bar alone this afternoon at about three o'clock."

"Yeah, three o'clock. What about Roberta?"

"Never mind."

Lila wanted to be with her own kind and left early, joining Sheena and Emily who were making plans for the Kitsch-Inn's contingent in the Gay Pride March. The year before, the Inn girls had become notorious for having walked the sixty blocks in prom dresses singing *Come on baby let the good times roll* over and over again. This year they were considering a march of mermaids.

"We could tie our feet together and hop all the way." Sheena said enthusiastically. "Helen Hayes can be the emcee and announce *These are the survivors of The Bermuda Triangle* when we get to the reviewing stand and no politicians are in it."

Lila didn't say anything, since she was still a novice when it came to the kitsch state of mind.

"What happened to our giant globe that said 'KITSCH' on it?" Sheena asked, obviously having moved on to a new concept.

"The mice ate it," Emily reported.

"Well, we can always go back to the original idea of being bathing beauties with machine guns. Now that would be nice."

"How about a float?" Lila suggested, suddenly feeling inspired, "A giant closet?"

"A closet?" Sheena asked. "Doesn't that sound a little grim?"

"Well, Isabel has been talking up this idea of Lesbian Shame Week."

Since no one could decide, they went to the former Polish Country-Western bar turned punk bar on First Avenue. The new owners changed the name to *Beirut* and decorated it with barbed wire. They hadn't gotten around to the juke box though, so the girls played *Ode to Billy Joe*, the Temptations and Santana, dancing around until a punk behind the bar turned on the TV, blasting a ball game.

"Has anyone seen Kitty recently?" Lila asked.

"Yeah," Sheena reported. "I went to visit her at her girlfriend's mansion on Fire Island. It's really beautiful there with ocean and beaches and hundreds of disco queens running around. Some of them are very hard to talk to because they don't know how to discuss anything. Kitty is spending a lot of time as a dresser for a drag show called *Viva Cherry Grove* about the history of Fire Island. The first scene has gay cavemen.

Then a gay George Washington sings *Don't Cry For Me Argentina*. She's crazy in a really great way. Remember last year when she turned The Inn into a church and we spent hours mashing Wonderbread to make the host?"

"Well, at least she gets a summer on Fire Island, which is more than I can see for the three baked apples sitting here." Lila often felt it was her duty to insert a sense of reality to these conversations.

"You'll see, wait until the march." Sheena was excited now. "New York faggotry and dykeness will come out in all its grandeur. Fifth Avenue will be ours. . ."

THIRTY-ONE

"**I** like it when you watch me eating you out," Emily said. "I know it sounds strange, but I like that you're absolutely sure of who is making you feel that way. I guess I want the most intimacy possible, even though the whole process makes me painfully shy. Sometimes it's like an evenly matched arm wrestle with myself to be able to look you fully in the eyes while I'm licking your cunt."

Lila, on the other hand, was turned on as much by the process as the act and was also entertained, especially at the sight of Emily's earnest nose poking out over her pubic hair. Plus, every once in a while, Emily would have trouble keeping her tongue going for very long and would take a tiny rest by sticking it out and moving her head back and forth to prevent lock jaw.

"There, that's better," Emily said, her face glistening. "I didn't eat my baby for three days and I was getting awfully hungry."

Then they hung out in bed until the conversation got serious, with Emily talking quietly about her own life. She saw it as a series of new places, aloneness and private rituals. Like stealing. She would go off by herself in whatever town her parents happened to have chosen for the moment, towards the local Penney's or Kresky's or Woolworth's, where she would carefully heist material, art supplies and, when available, good cloth. It was always something with which to make something else. Emily had cut every school she ever attended to sit in the various art rooms until, after trying out college for a minute, she fled university art studios for the safety of a room anywhere, where she could make whatever she wanted to, in silence.

First it was stealing, then it was leaving. She left because, as a child, she had to leave and because, as an adult, it was natural. She left when things were bad or boring or she was searching for a catharsis.

"Once I was angry at something and just took off in a bad way. I stopped at a rooming house sort of place because that's where my ride had dropped me off. I think it was a fight with my boyfriend, or something equally stupid. There was a bar on the ground floor of the house and all the locals used to come there to bore each other. One night, this one guy started talking to me. Quite a few times over that next week, he would come by to the bar and we would talk. Nothing revelatory, just conversation. Then, one night, he wanted to go out for a walk to the Seven Eleven, so I went along with it. We bought some cigarettes and walked back to the bar. Right before I went upstairs he said he wanted to show me something. It was a picture of Jesus. One of those three-dimensional postcards. He gave it to me. I held it for a minute, not knowing quite what he wanted and then he told me to turn it over. It was dark by then. Leaves and twigs were blowing around. The only light came from the Hamm's sign in the bar window. On the other side, Jesus was naked, with an erection, and a little girl was on her knees licking it. He laughed and laughed. All I could think was *You just had to be an asshole, didn't you*. It was the next night that I got raped."

Sometimes Lila would hold Emily in her arms after hours in a hot factory or after sweet loving and coming, and watch her sleep. Emily would sleep leaning against the wall with her arms over her head and the slope of her breast leading into the slope of her stomach, shining in the streetlight. Sometimes Lila would be making love to her playfully and kiss her so wetly, she'd lick her face.

"Don't do that," Emily would say, recoiling. "I don't mean anything against you, but please don't lick my face. When I was raped the first time he spit on my face. It's just not romantic for me, I'm sorry."

It was through making love with Lila that Emily showed more and more of her scars.

"Since then I try not to leave when things are bad." Emily's voice was very even, her pronunciation deliberate.

"It's taken on so much significance for me. I never know exactly why I go anywhere. People ask me that all the time, so I've learned that they need to hear a reason. But anything definite that I tell them is usually a lie. How can I explain what it's like to feel a new kind of weather for the first time to someone who lived with their parents until they were thirty? When people ask me, I just don't know what to say."

By this time they were wide awake and sat, wrapped in blankets, eating some old rice from the refrigerator. They ate as differently as they thought. Lila was quick and noisy, Emily precise and measured.

From Lila's point of view, Emily had vowed to live differently and so she did. Lila hadn't vowed anything at all but had done the same. Yet, Lila could see that they each retained huge chunks of the lives that they had left behind. For herself, it was her arrogance, believing that she had to right to live her life exactly the way she wanted to, no matter how laid back she felt like acting. In Emily's manners she saw a legacy of well-bred generations, which Emily said she cared nothing for, and a learned grace that Lila adored. Emily claimed it bored her.

Even though Emily tried to deny it, Lila found that there were things about her own ways that seemed distasteful to Emily. Like when Lila would enter an apartment as though she lived there, and walked room to room, touching things, pulling books off the shelves. Or when her friends would yell and scream at each other and five minutes later be laughing together as if nothing had happened. There were other things too. Like the way Lila ate.

"Lila, I know this is going to sound really crazy and after I say it you can forget about it, but I just want you to know how I feel. You're always telling me to talk about things that are on my mind, instead of keeping them in, so I'm going to tell you this. Please don't chomp when you eat. It makes me feel sick. Don't be angry at me baby, I love you so much."

"Just call me Noam Chompsky," Lila replied, smiling, but from then on she carefully checked to make sure that her mouth was closed whenever she found herself eating in Emily's presence, and that task made her feel unusually tired.

THIRTY-TWO

Gay Day finally came. The sky was teasingly grey but everyone knew that it never rained on the Gay Pride March. Lila stepped off the RR train at Columbus Circle, and it all came back in a wave of color. Who needed the Rainbow Gathering? It was right there on the sidewalks of New York. Fifty thousand homosexuals flaunted it that day, each having gone through their own personal weird shit and wild struggles to be proud. Even though they waved brilliant banners of soft colors and balloons and danced in the streets to samba music, gays are a very, very tough people.

Lila started out in the back, walking double-paced down Fifth so she could take turns marching with each contingent. This was her annual opportunity to be the generic lesbian.

"It's okay to be gay," she said to a Greek man selling sodas to thirsty fairies for two bucks each, "that's the theme for today."

In her Nina Hagen t-shirt, she marched and sang, offered a "Happy Gay Day" to every queen and stopped to exchange kisses with anyone who yelled out "I love Nina Hagen."

Lila marched with the Gay Psychologists and the Gay Bankers, Gay High-Tech workers and Gay Catholics. She walked with Gay Harvard Alumni, and the Eulenspiegel Society who, along with their affiliate, Gay Male Sadomasochism Activists, led each other by leashes past Tiffany's. She stood strong with Mirth and Girth, gays who like fat men, Gay Zionists, Gay Anti-Zionists and Gay Non-Zionists. She skipped the Gay Cops. Lila got militant with Gay Youth, chanting, "Two, Four, Six, Eight, How Do You Know Your Kids Are Straight?" She sat down with Gay Teachers to protest the Catholic War Veterans counter-demonstration at Saint Patrick's Cathedral. They were in uniform holding signs like "God Made Adam and Eve, Not Steve or Bruce." She cheered Grandmas for Gays and felt, yet again, overcome to the point of tears at the sight of Parents of Gays, with their handpainted signs, "We Love Our Gay Children." Lila boogied for blocks with a Latin percussion band surrounded by thousands of sweating faggots and dykes just dancing freely under the buildings of New York City. She sang *It's Raining Men* with the Gay Men's Chorus, screamed "US Out of Central America" with Black and White Men Together and chanted "Rainbow Power is on the Move" with the New Alliance Party. By the time she'd made it to the front of the march, where all the girls were, it was already Twentieth Street and time to relax with the smiling unaffiliated lezzies. One day a year they got cheered, just for being gay. These few hours of approval brought out the dignity and the beauty in each marching queer.

"Hey Helen." Lila ran up to Helen Hayes in all her bleached blonde self. "It's great to see you Helen. It's okay to be gay."

"Yeah, but only for today. Tomorrow back to the same old shit."

"Hi Lila."

"I don't believe we've met."

"Sure we have," said the attractive red-head in a purple lame evening gown. "I'm Nancy, remember? Helen's girlfriend."

"Oh my God, you've changed." Lila quickly recovered her composure. "Where's the green dragon tattoo and the axle grease?"

"Anything for a show," Nancy smiled, having proven one of

her many points.

They started walking together and Lila felt a little nervous somehow since she still had the feeling that, regardless of her change in hair color, Nancy liked to keep a close watch over things. The longer they walked, the closer Nancy got, until they were shoulder to shoulder as if some very serious and discreet conversation was about to take place. A little further on ahead Lila could see Emily in a pink bandana looking very gorgeous in her sleeveless denim jacket, on the back of which was written in matching pink letters, CONEY ISLAND BABY.

"I've heard about your latest romance," Nancy was saying, like it was some big secret. "On the grapevine. Emily told Helen that you two had been going out for a while and that she would take Helen's rejects anytime."

"That's nice."

"Tell me Lila, just between us. Does Emily know about you and Muriel?"

"Of course. But that's not a romance. That's just how Muriel and I are friends."

"Right, right," she said, nudging Lila rather sharply in the gut. "But, just between us, how do you handle two women at once, if you know what I mean?"

Emily and Helen looked so cute giggling and laughing together a few yards in front of them. Nancy wasn't bad, it was just that Lila had no idea of who Nancy was, and therefore couldn't imagine how to answer her questions. There were always those fuzzy areas to lesbian etiquette, like how intimate are you really with the girlfriend of someone you once tried to pick up?

"I'm only asking you this Lila, because Emily has been repressed for a long time about getting close to people and she deeply needs to be loved, but I don't want you to hurt her. Be sure not to hurt her."

"Okay, Nancy, since you brought it up, I promise not to hurt her. But really, I'm sure Emily can take care of herself. Besides, well, people always have oversimplified explanations for things."

"Well, have it your way," Nancy said, taken aback but keeping her stride. "Be responsible Lila, do you know what I mean by that? Always remember that the other person has feelings that you need to consider. That's all. I wasn't crazy about your tone of voice just now, but I'll let it pass."

Lila ran up to her Coney Island Baby and threw her arms around her. They were getting down to Christopher Street by this time, where the sidewalks were overflowing with screaming, cheering gay people of every color and degree of faggotry, waving and throwing kisses. Emily put her arms around Lila, holding her like she had never done before, hugging her waist like she was her one and only girlfriend on the streets of Gay Day USA. They ended up with the crowd by the Hudson River, leaning against a concrete divider on what was left of the Westside Highway, next to a platoon of cops with demo-duty and across the street from both the river and the Ramrod. They were transformed into two sixteen-year-old girls in cut-off t-shirts, making out by the highway on the edge of the city. Lila hung on to Emily's neck and kissed her face right there in front of all those cops, just the way girls in spandex french-kiss by the cigarette machine in every lesbian bar in America. Lila felt the power of that old street greaser attitude. This is my girlfriend and I have to honor and protect her. In return she will hold me openly in the street, sexy and daring. That was what Lila was thinking when the rain came and Emily took her home.

THIRTY-THREE

The next morning, like what was getting to be every morning, Lila got up with Emily at six, even though she herself didn't need to stagger into the office until ten. At first it was out of courtesy and then out of guilt at how hard Emily worked for her paycheck. But, after a while, it became a silent, groggy and pleasant habit. They would step into the shower together, each one yawning while the other stood under the meager faucet. Each one waited with a body full of soap, while the other rinsed off. Even after she was clean, Emily would stand absentmindedly in the shower waiting for Lila to finish. She just liked being next to her. After Emily put on her medium brown eyebrow pencil and Lila found her cigarettes, they would head off to breakfast. Coffee for Lila and coffee and an English muffin for Emily. It was the only thing in her life that she did systematically every morning, whenever possible.

"I'm not paying for this," Emily said that morning, "Because it's cold."

Even though Emily's zipper was held together by a safety pin, Lila thought she was seeing traces of her Republican blood.

"Oh, forget about it," Lila said.

Actually, Emily had no intention of carrying out her threat

because as soon as she said it, she didn't really care any more. Lila, however, had a different reaction.

"I've never been able to talk back to waitresses," she said. "I can't return things to stores. I have a problem when the culprit is your common man or woman on the street. I can cross police lines, but I can't send back a cold English muffin."

They politely paid their checks and Lila ate it anyway because it was simply too disgusting to waste food when so many people were starving on Ninth Street. Then Lila walked Emily to the RR and turned around towards home for a few more minutes of sleep before getting on the RR herself.

Whenever Lila put Emily on the train she would picture what Emily's day would be like at the factory. It was called the American Fabric Association, where Emily performed a variety of skilled physical labors forty to fifty hours a week for five dollars an hour. As a result of the long hours and low pay, the other workers were all Hispanic men with dubious green cards. Emily said that she probably could get a better paying job but she didn't really care that much. She wasn't sure of how to go about it and this one would do, she insisted, until she saved up enough money to take another trip.

At noon, the phone on Lila's desk rang. It was Emily.

"Oh Lila, my boss saw me at the march. He told me this morning. He said I looked pretty and happy. I feel so good, I'm ecstatic. I just wanted to tell you about it. I love you more than ever."

The office wasn't too busy so Lila let herself sit and replay in her mind a fantasy Emily had told her in her low smoky voice. It started with Emily cutting fabric. In her right hand she held a razor blade tightly and repeated long, straight strokes, like swimming, but over and over again. With each stroke she would get further and further into a dream of the day when she would take her love away to Hawaii, or Greece. Lila would like Hawaii, Emily said, out on the sand on Big Island. All you needed was some shelter for when it rained. The ground was so rich, the fruit just grew, everywhere. Emily would build a roof for her baby and they'd lie on the sand and watch the water between the sand and the horizon. In all that blue Emily would take Lila in her arms and make love to her on the white sand in the open air, free, in the middle of the day and Lila would eat her, watch the waves, suck the waves, stroke the sand and Emily would look up at the sky, so exciting.

But Lila couldn't push Emily's other realities out of her mind. At the same moment she could remember Emily's voice dragging out her stories after long days at work.

"When are you going to go out with me? Johnny asked me for the tenth time."

"What did you say?" Lila had asked.

"I said *never."* Emily imitated his whiny voice. *"When are you going to give me your phone number?* NEVER. I like working with Eduardo better than Johnny. Eduardo never asks me out. He does ask a lot of other questions though. The other day he said *Emmie, look, my wife is selling Tupperware.* And he handed me a catalogue. I told him he had picked the wrong person. I don't even own a plate. I don't even own a fork. *Not even a fork?* He couldn't believe it." Emily was smiling by that time, as though just having someone to tell this to made it better. "I told him that I never cook. I don't know how. I eat all my meals in restaurants." She had looked Lila in the eye. "I'm sorry baby, I promised myself that next time I'm going to tell him that my girlfriend cooks for me, since it is true. That would be the only dignified thing to do."

At four that afternoon Lila got another phone call at work. Vicki gave her that "don't chatter so much on my time" expression. It was Emily again, but her voice was solemn and heavy.

"It was all a joke," she said, almost crying. "Everyone was saying to each other all day *I saw you at the march, maricon.* Only I fell for it. I forgot to be careful one more time."

She sounded so upset, Lila decided to cut out early once again, even though she knew it would probably be the last straw. On the one hand she hated putting Vicki in this position, since, as office manager, she would undoubtedly fire her. But, on the other hand, Lila didn't give a flying fuck if she got fired anyway. As long as she had keys in her pocket she would be okay. It was only when you had no keys that your life was definitely out of hand. Lila got on the subway. There was one car with all the windows closed and that was the one that all the New Yorkers on board flocked to, because closed windows usually meant air-conditioning. All the other cars were populated by nodded-out junkies and tourists.

Sitting on the subway, Lila was struck by a series of ideas about Emily, about why she was so drawn to her. As her sweat began to cool and her thighs began to unstick she remembered all the times in her life, especially when she was young, when she was just wandering around, walking all night or being in the wrong place or ending up in no place. She was just walking around when everyone else seemed to have a place to go. All these years she had felt that she was the only girl in the world doing that guy-like thing. When women have no place to go they get married or kill themselves. Only guys walked around all night. Now though, she knew that back then, somewhere Emily had been walking around too.

Lila was sitting in front of the factory waiting for Emily to come out. She flashed anxiously on work one more time and then shrugged it off. Work should never keep you from living. There were other job possibilities. She could be a messenger again. Life in front of Emily's factory was the typical inner city industrial chaos of various men pushing various racks and stacks of things up and down the block with one hand and touching the body of every passing female with the other. After fifteen minutes, Lila took refuge inside the building, and by five-thirty decided it was time to liberate Emily from her usual stint of overtime without pay. When she got upstairs, she was surprised to find her at the front desk.

"Emily, what are you doing in reception?"

"I guess the boss couldn't take me using all the machinery correctly all day long. It was too virile for him to handle so he banished me to secretarial. I don't even know how to use this stuff. These machines have been blinking and beeping all day and I can't figure out which button is *hold*. It took me an hour to find the *on* button for the typewriter."

"Well, come on now, don't give him your free time on top of all of that."

"Okay, I'll be down in a minute."

Twenty minutes later she stepped out of the elevator. Her fifty cent earrings looked, somehow, quite divine, fashionable and extraordinary. A late-shift rack pusher patted her ass.

"When are you going to go out with me?"

"I told you I'm gay," she screamed with a sudden, sharp and all-encompassing anger.

Lila looked at her and realized that her anger was always present but only showed itself when Emily was touched by the wrong person or at the wrong time or in some other way found her dignity to be under assault again.

"I'm going home to be with my girlfriend, pigfucker."

But he just laughed.

"I look into the future," Emily said that night, tired and sore but not admitting it, "and I see nothing, nothing at all. I know I'll travel, but aside from that I have no ambition and no fear."

"What about for yourself though? For your personality? I mean, Emily, aren't there things about yourself that you want to see change or develop or at least an expectation or two?"

"I want to go through the day without thinking about myself," she answered blandly. "From one thing to another. I want to talk to this person, make this thing, eat this food. I don't need drama. I don't think it's groovy anymore."

Before she fell asleep, Emily made little noises, like groans. They were calmer, more guttural versions of her own sex sounds and then she would quiver. The quiver told Lila that Emily had fallen asleep. For the next few moments Lila looked out the window into the La Mama costume shop. At that moment she promised herself that she would never betray this woman. She wanted to be the person in Emily's life who let her believe in love. Lila listened to the cats scurry and felt Emily's sleep sounds. Those images were imbedded permanently into her imagination.

THIRTY-FOUR

"Hello Arthur? Is Lacy home? This is Lila Futuransky calling."

"Hi Lila. Well, she's here but she's sort of busy. There's this fancy lady sitting in our living room who is trying to convince Lacy that she needs an agent. Wait a minute, hold on, here she comes."

"Hi Lila."

"Hi Lacy, Arthur says you're being recruited to the ranks of those with representation."

"Yes, yes, yes. I don't want to talk too loud, she's in the bathroom. Well, first she told me that *the only difference between artists who make it and artists who don't is promotion.* Then, later she said *if they read you once they'll read you twice.* I know I need an agent to protect me from publishers but who do you call to protect you from agents? Oh-oh she's finished shitting, bye honey, here's Arthur."

"Hello Arthur?"

"Yeah?"

"I just wanted to know when Sally Liberty was coming back. I need to talk to someone who has just taken a big trip."

"There are too many people taking trips around here if you

ask me," he said in one of those *you know what I'm talking about* voices.

"Not egos, Arthur, geography. You know, like a journey or a voyage."

"Lila, when you get a chance, you stop by here and see my most recent painting. It's a concave sunset and a convex sunrise so that night and day cave into each other in black and white paint and cigarette packages, to show the passage of time. It'll take you on a trip alright. You hang on now. Bye."

Lila had been reading and re-reading *On The Road*, she was almost through. But the closer she got to those final pages, the more doubts creepy crawled into her mind. She shared Jack's vision of women as sexual treasures and mystical beings who come in and out of your life like Arthur's suns, but there were still questions that Jack never touched on. Like, what do you do once you get to know them? He never stayed around long enough for that. All of this was why she had been seriously considering taking a trip somewhere, just to remember that Lila would be Lila wherever she was standing and it didn't have to be on those four square blocks below Fourteenth Street surrounded by those same old girls. She needed to take a trip like Jack's. But, then again, maybe it would be different for a woman. Maybe it didn't require a road at all.

"Let's pretend we're jumping in that pick-up truck and going out on the highway," she said to Emily. But Emily wasn't interested in that.

"I don't need an adventure everyday," she said.

Still, it was sticking in Lila's mind to take a trip.

"Buddy, you can't leave," Isabel implored as they shared her shift meal of Shepherd's Pie at Burger Heaven. She hadn't been fired yet. The lunch rush crowd was gone except for some old afternoon drinkers watching the Yankee game at the bar.

"Miss Subways, I need you—what about The Worst Performance Festival? It's coming up real soon."

"I wouldn't be gone for too long. Isabel, in some way, you're the one who understands me best. I know this because when you talk I agree so often that I don't need you to listen to me, you know it all already. Isabel, here, I am giving you my copy of *On The Road*. It is my gift to you."

"Buddy, I need you to write a scene for me, a trial. I don't really know what I want exactly but something about me dying and going to heaven, which is Grossinger's Hotel in the Catskills. First, though, naturally I have to be judged. The question is—have I really kept my integrity, or did I not sell out because no one was willing to buy? Can you picture a sort of Henry Fonda-Kafka-Job thing? Know what I mean?"

Somehow through the wonders of interpersonal communication, Lila did know what she meant. In fact, she was suddenly inspired and insisted at that very moment that they run off into the heat of midtown, over to The Jewish Division of the Public Library on Forty-Second Street to look at a very special thing right away.

The Jewish Room, being on the first floor of the giant main library building, had easy access and so became a resting place for those homeless men and women who were the inmates of the open wards of the city. Usually this room was noisy, smelled bad and was inhabited by a combination of religious Jews reading ancient texts and bag-ladies tearing up copies of *The New York Post*. Both sat there, rocking back and forth and talking to themselves. In the summer, it was hot and the windows were wide open, letting in the roar of the center city hustle outside. Two men collected money for a Black Museum that existed only in their dreams. Drug dealers promised Thai sticks, when it was only Mexican Cocoa-Cola buds. The Unification Church Missionaries, known as Moonies, drew diagrams explaining life and God with red and blue magic markers on portable boards. A bad saxophone player repeated over and over the theme song from *The Odd Couple* and then the theme song from *The Pink Panther*. All this drifted into The Jewish Room.

"The guy's name was Peretz," Lila told Isabel, looking through a fat card catalogue. "See how many cards are in his section? There's even a street named after him, right near us on Houston and First. Only nobody's ever heard of the guy. Here's the story I was telling you about. It's called *Bonche Schweig*."

They politely put in their request and waited for the cute librarian to fetch the book.

"You see Isabel, it's like this. All these guys were writing, and women too, writing in Yiddish and trying out different ideas, forms, like writers anywhere. They had enthusiastic readers, critics, schools taught their books. Then came the war and their subject matter, their readers and their language was practically destroyed. Imagine sitting in a kitchen on Mosholu Parkway realizing that your career and your art form disappeared because your readers had been killed."

"I never thought about it that way before," Isabel said. "It reminds me in a way of when I saw this exhibit of Russian painters from 1900-70. First they were doing what everybody else was doing, except in their own Russian way. There was impressionism, cubism, all that. You're walking along the exhibit and all of a sudden there's a painting of an orange tractor with Lenin standing on it. History changes and the artist goes out of business."

The librarian came over with their book and gave them both a big smile. Isabel read it then and there while Lila watched her react. It was about a guy named Bonche who never had a good moment in his whole life. People would shit all over him and he consistently took it. What was more important, from Peretz' point of view, was that no matter what happened, Bonche never said anything bad against God. When he died, he had to be judged in the heavenly court. The defense attorney proved that no matter how much he suffered, Bonche had never cursed God. The court decided that since he died without having done anything wrong, Bonche won the trial and could have anything he wanted in all imagination. That was his reward. God would give him whatever he asked for.

"What I want," said Bonche, "is, everyday, a hot roll with some fresh butter."

Then, said Peretz, the prosecutor broke out laughing. That was the end of the story.

"You get it Isabel?" Lila was hysterical with enthusiasm. "In the end, the prosecutor really won. Bonche was turned into such a schmuck from never tasting anger or desire or revenge that when his moment finally came, his spirit was too dead to be able to do anything about it."

"Isabel," Lila asked over an ice cream soda at Howard Johnson's. "What's the difference between being stagnant and being stable?"

"Stagnant is what someone else wants you to be, stable is what you need them to be."

"Isabel, when God tells you that you can have anything you want, what are you going to ask for?"

"I don't know." Isabel answered, scratching her head. "I wouldn't want to get any of the things that I want too suddenly, because then the fun and the search and the dreams would all be over. It's not the satisfaction I'm after. I like thinking about new ways of doing things and then making up shows about the trying. Do you think God could give me something like that?"

"You've already got that."

"Oh, yeah. Well, how about health insurance?"

THIRTY-FIVE

Twice in one week, Lila got mistaken for a prostitute. She was walking home on Chrystie Street in the middle of the afternoon through Chinatown's warehouse district and two trucks drove by.

"Going out? Going out?"

She decided it was an honest mistake. Why else would a woman be walking down the street wearing a shoulder bag?

The next day she was on the corner of Tenth Street and Third Avenue waiting to make a phone call when a guy drove up in a cab.

"Hey you. Get in," he yelled out the window.

"I'm not a prostitute," Lila said. "She's a prostitute," pointing to a woman standing next to the phone booth.

"Oh," he said, shifting his gaze. "Hey you. Get in."

Then Lila got mistaken for a racist. Sal Paradise took her out to hear Ron Carter and then they went to Maureen's bar to play her juke box. Maureen had a Gertrude Stein haircut and a figure to match. She also had a great collection of forty-fives like Dinah Washington, Peggy Lee, Frankie crooning *Witchcraft*, very atmosphere-y. Everything got ruined though, when this man at the bar decided it was time to impose himself on the general mood with his fucking presumptions.

"I work in a shoe store waiting on filthy rich people. Like, you know basketball stars, Lionel Ritchie, Herb Alpert, the tops. Those ball pros are the worst, let me tell you. The way I figure it, they would be spending their lives shooting hoops in school yards and turning into muggers if they hadn't hit the big time. They just piss all over themselves watching a white guy tie their shoes."

People don't look closely enough. They see tits and assume they're for sale. They see white skin and think they're among friends.

"I don't see it that way," Sal said. "I don't want to take away from you that you're working hard and rich people are being rude to you because that's real and it hurts. But it's success that makes people snotty, not their blackness. Maybe you could think about it again."

So, of course, the guy had to fall all over himself to justify the unjustifiable with references to "ignorant people," meaning someone other than himself. Lila just faded out and thought about MTV.

That very night she got mistaken for straight.

"Hey doll," the same guy at the same bar called out to a woman sitting alone in the corner. "Want me to walk you home?"

"Why don't you walk me home?" Sal said, trying to divert the guy's attention.

"Oh of course darling, lispen to me suger." The bar sitter flapped his wrists expecting, of course, that swish-baiting was just fine with everyone. It was another example of a typical American asshole who wouldn't know an emotion if it walked up and punched him in the eye.

Lila and Sal split immediately, feeling sorry for Maureen, who had to serve the creep for the rest of the night. They went to the Polish Country-Western bar turned Beirut turned gay men's fuck bar called The Manhole. God, things changed quickly as of late. The place still had a good juke box. There was

Psychedelic Shack and *Tell Me What I Say*. Half way through getting drunk and singing their selections, chatting with the leather-clad clientele and having a great time, Lila realized that she and Sal were going to go home together and have sex with each other. Surprisingly the thought didn't bother her or Sal one bit. So that's exactly what they did. There was no fucking or anything like that, since even before her voyage into lesbos, Lila the het had never liked fucking, she didn't have the stomach for it. But they played with old-fashioned sweaty boy and girl stuff, easy and light with a lot of energy. It was all vaguely reminiscent and fun, but most importantly, Lila found out that her pal Sal knew how to make love to a woman and it made her respect him all the more.

THIRTY-SIX

Emily was hard at work at The Kitsch-Inn, and Lila was trying, in her klutzy way, to help. The Inn had a new policy of putting on a fully produced play every weekend. This meant that Mondays they came up with a new idea, Tuesdays they wrote the scripts. Wednesdays were for blocking and costumes and late night set construction. Thursday was reserved for full-dress and tech rehearsal, and Friday and Saturday were for performances. Sunday there was always a party.

Even though she thought the shows were creative and charming, Lila's personality was much more suited to Isabel Schwartz' personal philosophy of theatre. This approach emphasized mulling over, developing, rehearsing and publicizing and then performing enough times so the show could become itself. Whenever Isabel did her shows, she would spend weeks before rehearsing, and after that, handing out flyers in lesbian bars, asking each woman individually if she would please come. Her approach was based on the idea that most lesbians in lesbian bars are never asked to come to anything that is made expressly for them. Usually this approach had some effect, but fairly frequently Isabel would be outside at the last minute, in costume and make-up, standing on Saint Mark's Place asking dykie-looking women in restaurants to please come to her show, offering to hold the curtain until they finished eating. She even gave drug dealers free passes on very slow nights.

The Kitsch girls, on the other hand, were less concerned with who and how many came to the shows. The theatre was so small and the casts so large that there wasn't much room for the audience anyway. Besides, spontaneity was the name of the game, and they relished being known as the "girls who would do anything." Somewhere each one of them privately suspected that if they got too organized they might turn mean, and each one knew how mean mean girls could be. So they kept it light, non-competitive and without an ounce of desperation.

Lila loved watching Emily develop her weekly creations out of nothing. The night before costume day, they would walk the streets for an hour or so. Emily would look around and suddenly seize upon a piece of old cardboard or some dirty clothing or a thrown away board, all from garbage cans and vacant lots and carry it back to the Inn.

"If I didn't think theatre could be made from garbage, I wouldn't be doing theatre," she liked to say once in a while.

Her budget for that week's production was six dollars and fifty cents, raised by auctioning off a bowling shirt. They had been working most of the evening when Sheena walked in with aqua-marine hair and a shirt saying "SLUT" in sequins.

"Hi Sheena."

"Hi Slut."

"I beg your pardon?"

"It's my new attitudinal band, *The Macho Sluts.* I need some people to be in it with me, so I'm holding open auditions. Anyone who answers to the name SLUT, is in."

"Well forget it." Lila already had enough no-future projects, especially with the Worst Performance Festival coming up so soon.

"Sheena," Lila said, without looking up from trying to thread a needle, "what's it like outside? We've been in here for hours."

"Well," Sheena reflected, chomping on some organic potato

chips, "the streets are filled with Michael Jackson imitators."

"Hey Sheena, you want to help me?" Emily called out from under a pile of junk.

"Sure Slut."

"Here I'm doing the new set for the show this weekend. Cast of thirty, all in period costumes. We're turning the Inn into The Triangle Shirtwaist Factory and I need fifty cutouts of sewing machines."

"Groovoid. How long is the run?"

"Two nights, the usual."

"Groovoid."

"I don't mean to interfere, girls," Lila injected, looking for a band-aid for her overpricked finger, "but why do you do all this chaotic work for one weekend when, if you would prolong your runs a little, the shows could get better and more people could see them. I mean don't you have any ambition?"

"No," they said in unison as Sheena started cutting sewing machines out of an old box of Tide.

Just then Kitty appeared in the doorway, her eyes red and puffy, clutching a small carrying bag. Emily crawled out from under her props to embrace her friend.

"What happened? Come in, what's the matter, Kitty?"

They all retreated to The Inn's beat-up couch while Kitty cried and shook with sorrow. Emily sat on her lap, Lila handed tissues and Sheena offered her organic potato chips. They each tried in their own way to show their friend that she was home.

"I left her," she said, blowing her nose. "We had a fight coming back from Gristede's. I offered to carry her bags but she didn't want me to. I offered to make her a drink, but she didn't want it. I asked her if she wanted me to leave and she said she didn't know. Everytime I asked her something she rolled up tighter and tighter into a ball and crawled deeper into the bed. I felt she didn't want to be in the same co-op with me."

"Maybe you asked her too much stuff?" Sheena said shyly.

"But I want her to ask me," she wailed, "I want her to ask me to do every little thing for her, to show me that she needs me."

"You know Slut, one thing you gotta get together in your head is that each person can only go so far. If you pressure them to go farther still, they're going to hate you. Just take what you can get. Have some more potato chips."

They talked more and took turns walking around the block with Kitty and deciding where she was going to stay that night. This went on until a white BMW drove up to The Inn and Kitty's face lit up with the joyful confirmation of being loved. She waved good-bye to her friends and climbed into the front seat.

Sheena, Emily and Lila sat in silence for a moment, each reflecting, in her own peculiar frame of reference, on the weird situations people get themselves into in the name of love. Then, one by one, they resumed the task of cutting out sewing machines from old boxes of detergent and mounting them on old wire hangers.

"The whole thing makes me think," Sheena said, "that sometimes love means finding out more about yourself than you ever really wanted to know."

Emily was busy gluing and didn't pay attention, so only Lila agreed.

THIRTY-SEVEN

Friday morning Lila woke up with Emily at six o'clock and found a small gift box lying on her stomach.

"What's this?"

"A good luck present for the Worst Performance Festival tonight."

Lila opened the box. Inside was a black lace brassiere with an underwire and a little pink flower stitched in between the cups. Next to it sat black lace underpants with another stitched pink rose. She shut the box quickly, and opened it again, slowly, to look more closely.

"Are you embarrassed?" Emily asked.

No. It was intimate, so involved with Lila's secret life that she was thrilled to the teeth.

"The right size and everything."

Lila imagined Emily standing thoughtfully at the counter, fingering the bras, deciding which one she would buy.

"I know my baby's breasts."

"I know you do."

The house was packed that night for the Worst, which was the third act on a bill at AVANT-GARDE-ARAMA, a former Ukranian restaurant turned performance club. Fortunately for

Lila, Isabel and Company, the opening piece was a woman eating a grapefruit and the following was a man walking around in a circle with a paper bag over his head talking about how much he liked to pee before going on stage. All the girls were there, except for Muriel, who was sunning herself somewhere on the Costa del Sol.

The lights came up on Helen Hayes and Mike Miller, the administrative heavy of the ARAMA. They were sitting at a panel-like table with official looking nameplates. Suddenly Lila rushed out into the crowd in tight black pants and a tight black t-shirt that said "Soon To Be A Major Homosexual."

"Good evening ladies and friends. I will be your emcee for this evening and I am pleased to be with this special audience. Who else but you, people who pay five dollars to come see this kind of work, could be better qualified to pick the worst performer of 1984? But first, before we begin, I want to remind you that all of us here together tonight, well, we are a community, a community of enemies. And we have to stay close to each other so we can watch out and protect ourselves. To give you an idea for the criteria by which to judge the participants, we have an excerpt from last year's winner, Amy Cohen. I will now read to you from her prize-winning text, *Artificial Turtle*:

Inside out. Empty Box as silence.
Empty box as monument to. . . emptiness.

"Isn't that just awful?"
The audience, getting into the groove, booed wildly, then, pleased with themselves, applauded and cheered. Isabel had promised Lila that they would. She understood the simple fact that people like to be insulted in public because they think it means they're important.

"Tonight we are proud to introduce our panel of minor celebrity judges from competing cliques to vote down each other's friends. First, representing the girls, from the Kitsch-Inn, The Platinum Angel herself, Helen Hayes."

Helen was dressed to her divaish teeth.

"It's simply terrible to be here tonight."

"Thank you, tell us Helen, how was your show at Dance-a-teria last night?"

"Pretty bad, pretty bad. I think it would have been competitive in this festival."

"That's great Helen, isn't she swell ladies and gentlemen? Thanks doll. And now, representing the boys, the Avant-Garde's head cheerleader, Mike Miller. Hey Mike, I love your beard. Thank you and enjoy the show."

Lila and Isabel had agreed before hand that Mike would have no lines and no microphone. Those boys talked too much anyway. As he sat there looking stupid, Helen announced the first entry.

"Our opening act tonight will be East Village Performance Artist Isabel Schwartz with her piece, *My Brilliant Career*, improvisational ruminations on nothing."

Isabel entered in her pink baseball pants, yellow sneakers and black sunglasses.

"Look, I don't have anything to say to you and you don't have anything to say to me," she sighed, looked as bored as possible, like she was too big for Carnegie Hall. "I don't even like you. I thought about coming here with the slides of my lesbian honeymoon at Grossinger's, but we're only getting ten dollars for this performance, so why waste a good idea for ten dollars? Instead, I'll read to you from my reviews. *Isabel Schwartz is a Genius, Isabel Schwartz is a whiz on stage, Isabel Schwartz is witty and exuberant.* That's all you deserve. Good-bye."

"Well," said Helen, "That was pretty terrible. Very annoying at times. It's going to be tough to beat. *Dance Magazine* called our next performer, *an actor with the wit, personal style and glamour of a young Dustin Hoffman.* Will you please welcome Ratso Tootsie."

Roberta walked calmly onto the stage, scratching her head, dragging her robes and drinking a beer. She took a cassette tape out of her pocket and dropped it on the floor. Then she took out a box of slides and tossed them uncaringly in the air. Finally she unraveled a film all over the stage. She finished the beer, spit on the floor and left.

"Thank you Ratso," said Helen, with an impeccable display of dishonest politeness. "The slides were very experimental but I found the film slightly opaque. Our next performer Patty Dyke uses time and space to interpret the self, herself, in all its post-modern incarnations. Patty's influences include Artaud, Rimbaud, Van Gogh, The Go-Go's and Uncle Ho."

It was Isabel again. This time she was dressed in a pink and green bath towel. She was plugged into a walkman and danced to the music that no one else could hear. But when the chorus came on, she screamed out, "Beat it, just beat it," and hit herself on the head with a stick. Helen, looking properly upset, tried to ease her off the stage, but Isabel, being the prototype horrible performer, started making a scene.

"I've given you everything," she shouted, running up to a stunned and silent Mike and pulling his beard, "everything, and you just fucked me in the ass you dumb prick," and then she threw off the towel.

After intermission, when the audience had calmed down, the lights came up slowly on the final segment of the show, "The Lesbian Nuns and Their Dirty Habits: The Real True Story (With Carlos)." There were Lila, Isabel and Roberta dressed as nuns with incense and chanting and holy water and Bach organ music played in slow motion in the background. The three of them were mumbling "Domini, Domini" and spraying holy water on everyone. When they finished their procession, each one assumed a pose in a different shadow and put on their name plates. Lila was "Sister Roger," Roberta, "Sister Fresnel," and Isabel, "Sister Bruce Weber."

Helen announced "The Flying Nun" and Lila pouted, slapped her thigh and said, "Come on Carlos, we've got to think of a way to save the convent. I know, a bake sale!" To which Helen, chomping on a cigar replied, "But Seester." Lila held on to her habit and made a few Gidget type moves to get ready for take-off.

Reading from her index cards Helen announced sister number two, Julie Andrews.

Roberta plastered a big smile on her face and began to teach the audience to sing Do-Re-Mi, until, right in the middle of *Me, a name I call myself*, she yelled out "Stop, stop. This is a sham. When I was a kid I was in love with Julie Andrews. I had her picture on my mirror. I dressed like her, I had a Julie Andrews wallet. My mother took me to all her movies. One day I got the address of her fan club and I wrote her a long letter. Julie, I said, Julie I love you, I love you. And do you know what she did, that bitch? She sent me back an autographed picture. I cried for days, my mother tried to console me with a Julie Andrews coloring book. Then Halloween came, and she took me to Woolworth's tempting me with a Mary Poppins costume but I said no. You know why? Do you know why? Because I didn't want to be Julie Andrews. I wanted to have Julie Andrews."

"And now," announced the lovely Helen Hayes, "Sister number three, The Singing Nun." At which point Isabel whipped out an electric guitar and started singing "Dominique." The others joined in. Unfortunately, they hadn't rehearsed this part of the show and none of them knew the lyrics so they just kept singing "Dominique-ah, nique-ah, nique-ah" over and over again until The Flying Nun took off, the Singing Nun switched to Hound Dog and Julie Andrews started making out with a woman in the first row.

Finally Helen had the foresight to turn out the lights. So went the Worst Performance Festival. Oh, well, that's show biz.

THIRTY-EIGHT

I t was a lazy morning and Lila and Emily were lying around in bed, with no where in particular that either needed to go.

"Lila, I'm so happy to be with you that I can't believe it sometimes. Just being in your presence somehow calms so many of my sorrows. I like feeling sexy, that I'm attractive to you, but it doesn't make me want to sleep around or anything like that. I know you want me to stay open to other women, and I'm trying, but for now I'd rather just think of you as my baby. Sometimes I wish people weren't so obsessed with sex in such distorted ways. Then there would be more energy for looking at how beautiful the earth is."

"I know what you're saying," Lila whispered, kissing Emily's neck, "But for me there's something incredible about two people getting it together to touch each other. I've learned so much about myself by having sex with different people, or just from finding out how someone does it. The dangerous part is when you use sex to justify hurting someone. That's the problem."

Like anyone who suddenly finds themselves in the presence of a compatible imagination, Lila perceived and felt daily occurrences with an insight beyond her own capability. When she was confronted by a more complex place of understanding, she knew it was not her interpretation alone but that of she and Emily together. Lila did not know if Emily would find this pathetic or wonderful. At the same time Lila began to feel a combination of panic and delight at watching someone be transformed by her love for them. But she had a more tentative enthusiasm for her own changes. Emily wanted the bulk of Lila's attention, which meant behaving a way that Lila had never even dreamed of behaving. Lila was learning a new way to live, where someone else had something to say about the decisions that she made in her own life. In fact, she'd never even had another person know so much about where she was everyday. She was trying it out half through resolve and half through an unclear kind of intimidation. Combined with her real love for Emily was the threat that Lila really wasn't a good person, that she was capable of all the abandonment and exploitation that Emily had experienced from others, and Lila was determined to prove that Emily's fears would never be justified.

The flesh around Emily's nipples was soft and wrinkled. There was enough give for Lila to play absent-mindedly, folding Emily's nipples into her skin.

"I think I admire that about you Lila, a little bit anyway. You desire someone and you try to live it out. It's too intimate for me, touching another person's body. That's why I haven't had as much experience as you, it's sharing your fantasy with someone. I mean, I have a lot of fantasies about women, but not about having sex, more like imagining doing things with them, having them in my life."

As Lila started to lick the softness under Emily's breast, they both felt the comfort. It had been a long time since Lila had been running out on the street all night, alone, figuring things out, chasing girls and conversation, but she didn't miss it that much because something special and sweet had come into her life. Maybe it was a gift to remind her that it was right to believe in love.

"I know I've fallen in love with you, Lila. I've been celibate for a long time, you know, but today at work I was thinking about how much I like having you as my girlfriend."

"Oh, you like having a woman pay attention to you and take care of you and make love to you? How unusual."

"Lila, I need to ask you something kind of strange."

"Sure babe."

"When you answer the phone on a phone machine and it's ringing, the light flashes on, right?"

"Yeah."

"So, if you need to put it on hold, you press down the hold button and the light starts blinking. If you want to speak to that person, do you press the hold button again?"

"No. After you press hold it pops up blinking silently. When you want to talk you press the blinking one."

"Thanks darlin'."

"Sure. Now I have a question for you. Why do you scotch tape your bangs to your forehead every morning before you get dressed and then take off the tape before you got out? Not that I think it's weird or anything, I'm just curious."

"That way my bangs will lie flat like Audrey **Hepburn in** *Charade*."

"Oh well, in that case."

Lila thought Emily was the cutest thing. She was at times prehistoric and then, suddenly, more Dior than Dior. But, even with her sophisto fancies, she had been in the world of needle and thread for so long that she hadn't caught up with even the most basic technologies, aside from industrial machinery of course. Like an intercom, for example. Lila watched her struggle for ten minutes one morning in Lila's apartment, trying to figure out how to buzz in Sheena, who was coming back from a visit to her mother on Avenue X in south Brooklyn. Emily tried to talk through the listen button and not press the talk button and then she couldn't hear who it was because the listen button wasn't pressed. Sheena got in though, because the downstairs lock was broken.

"What a place," she said, scratching the newly shaved part of her partially shaved head. "Everyone who stays there is crazy. They don't know why they're there but they don't know the names of any other places, and everyone is divorced by the time they're nineteen. But I did do some serious thinking about my future. I'm going to give myself one more year to find people to be in the *Macho Sluts* and then another year to see if we make it. If nothing happens I'll be a fireman, uh, person."

At least something was settled. They invited Sheena to go out for a walk but she had to run off to meet her friend Jenny who was supposed to have some information about a women's circus brigade in Nicaragua.

Emily and Lila went out anyway, strolling hand in hand through Washington Square Park. Lila saw all the drug dealing going on and remembered that she hadn't seen Ray for a long time, hoping that he wasn't in trouble or something more serious than that.

"Lila, I was watching you talk to Sheena and everything she said seemed to make sense to you. I realized that everything everyone says seems to make sense to you, which made me think that you must be fairly bizarre. And I must be equally bizarre to not have noticed for so long. I feel like I've been walking around the world, flying around it, like some character in Rocky and Bullwinkle who has a rocket attached to his leg. But now, I've been feeling love from you and all of a sudden, I'm paying attention."

On the way back they stopped every now and then for small kisses, and then for some gelatti. Not from the place that had fired Tina. The boss claimed she'd had too many visitors and couldn't keep her mind on the gelatti. Instead they stopped in at one of the many competitors on the same block.

"Oh look, they have the flavor *fig*. That's the same word as *cunt* in Italian."

So, of course they ordered fig and sat on a car in front of Lila's building to eat it slowly because it was so, so sweet. Lila rubbed her fingers over the nape of Emily's neck, through her dyed hair and then, at the same moment, they both keyed into the conversation going on behind them.

"That's gay liberation. They think they can do whatever they want whenever they want it."

About five men were drinking beer across the street and talking very loudly, obviously intending to be heard.

"You want to try it. Come on and try it sister. I've got A BIG COCK. See *mamacita*, I'd love to fuck your cunt."

Lila didn't want to go upstairs, because she didn't want them to see where she lived. They started walking slowly away, but the men followed.

"Come on you cunt, I bet you've got a nice pussy, you suck each other's pussy's right? I'll show you a cock that you'll never forget. . . ."

For Lila, this was a completely normal though unnecessary part of daily life. As a result she had learned docility, to keep quiet and do a shuffle, to avoid having her ass kicked in. Emily, however, exploded in a combination of offended innocence and righteous anger.

"Fuck you faggot spic."

Lila immediately pulled her into the building, trembling and overcome by layers of different reactions.

"Emily, Emily, listen to me. I don't want to tell you not to fight because you're right to fight, but once you get queer-bashed, it comes back to you over and over again because no one's going to be on your side. I don't want to tell you not to be angry Emily but please, don't say *spic*."

"I don't mean that against Spanish people," she said, after a moment of silence. "Out there are two men who tortured me for no other reason than that they felt like it. I'm going to kill a man someday. I'm sure I'm going to kill a man."

They sat upstairs in the dark, making feeble attempts to talk. The sounds of the men, drunker and laughing, came in through the open window.

"If I wasn't a lesbian," Emily said, looking out from behind the curtain, "I would be insane today. You know my rapes have changed me. You know better than anybody else that there are things I can't do sexually because they make me sick. I know you want to put your fingers inside me, I know you want to lick my face, someday you're going to reject me for that. You're going to get bored, I know it."

"Emily, what are you talking about. I love making love with you, we have a very deep friendship. Let's just calm down here and sit a minute."

"Don't condescend to me." Emily was walking back and forth around the tiny apartment. Lila had no idea what to do so she started smoking cigarettes, one after the other.

"I'm not groovy like you Lila, like you and your friends. This woman, that woman, this woman, that woman and a man. When is Muriel coming back? You haven't mentioned her for a while. I think it's a little disgusting to tell one lover about sex you had with someone else."

"What are you talking about?"

"*Fica ussatte.*"

"What the hell does that mean?" Lila was freaking out. She had absolutely no idea of what to do. The room was filling with smoke. Emily was pacing harder and harder and Lila couldn't imagine a way out of the whole thing.

"What does it sound like?"

"I don't understand Italian. You know that."

"It means *used cunt.*"

Lila was so surprised at how quickly everything had gotten out of hand that the only emotion she felt in touch with was a desire for the entire episode to be over. Emily's mouth got very smooth and tight. They were still for a minute and it seemed to Lila that Emily was dancing around the room and her emotions were a burst of colors that had all run into each other until they were muddy and brown.

"I'm sorry Lila, do you want me to go away?"

"No. Emily, just because we're having a fight doesn't mean that you have to go away. Why don't you sit down next to me, okay?"

"I'm sorry Lila, you know I get so tired from working with those guys hassling me all day long. When I won't go out with them they start talking about pussy right in front of me, and how they're going to go out and get some. I think if they knew I ate pussy for breakfast they would be pretty humiliated."

Lila tried to laugh, hoping everything would be better now.

"I'm driving you away from me," Emily said after a pause. "I'm driving you away when you love me because I'm afraid that if you leave me I'll be raped again. I'm safe when I walk down the street with you. Even if we get scared sometimes. I've been totally alone in strange places for so long. I don't want to walk alone anymore."

"Emily, listen, who gets raped, it's all haphazard. It could have been me instead of you. I haven't been raped yet but it doesn't mean I won't be."

"Pig-fuckers," Emily blurted out. "I won't let anybody hurt my baby."

Lila walked in the streets like someone who had always walked in the streets and for whom it was natural and rich. She walked with the illusion that she was safe and that the illusion would somehow keep her that way.

Yet, that particular night as she went out for cigarettes, Lila walked uneasily, her mind wandering until it stopped of its own accord, on the simple fact that she was not safe. She could be physically hurt at any time and felt, for a fleeting moment that she would be. She sat on a trunk of a '74 Chevy and accepted that this world was not hers. Even on her own block. She sat on that Chevy watching a young man pick through a garbage can, a young woman sell her shoes, fancy uptown diners in a Szechuan restaurant and a German tourist taking pictures of it all. Lila was full of questions about the power of defiance and its limitations.

PART FIVE

THIRTY-NINE

"**W**e were a hit buddy," Isabel was telling her over and over again. "The Worst Performance Festival was a hit. Isn't that pathetic? Critics were there and they actually liked us insulting them and telling them they were full of shit. It worked even better than we wanted it to. After all the good shows we've done, I can't believe we're getting reviews for that."

They walked out of the xerox store with copies of the first five scenes of *Job Revisited*.

"I'm sorry Isabel, I'm just not with it today. No, you're right. It's utterly sickening and predictable."

"By the way Miss Subways, that Kerouac book you gave me, there's something weird about it, like it has a magic power. Even though I hated the main guy, by page three I wanted to be him. I used to see that book in my brother's room when I was little, but I never opened it. Look at this."

She pulled a crinkled piece of newspaper out from her purple pockets.

"It says here that he died in his forties watching the Galloping Gourmet on TV in his mother's house. He was living with his mother and drinking beer all day long. Funny huh, how the author has nothing to do with the book. But even knowing what kind of person wrote this doesn't make its effect on me any different. I guess the road is the only image of freedom that an American can understand."

Lila couldn't answer. She went for a walk in Tompkins Square Park. Everything was so much more difficult than she'd thought. Which was better, the sad truth or the fun deception?

She saw Linda Casbah sitting with baby Jane and went over to help rock the stroller. Linda had her own analysis of this topic of sex, art, travel and success.

"I want to do a serious show about gender changes," she said, seriously. "When I was an underground go-go star, everyone wanted to interview me. I was invited to rich people's parties. They even brought me on tour to Amsterdam where somehow the Dutchies became convinced I was a transsexual and kept referring to me as *he*. I'd never been so in before. When I got pregnant though, and decided to live with John, everyone dropped me suddenly, like pregnancy was impossibly passé. Linda Casbah the transsexual go-go dancer is a lot sexier than mommy."

Her child at eight months old had that brand new skin that turned red when you touched it. She talked on and on in a happy series of garbled baby sounds.

"Pretty soon I'm going to find out what she has to say for herself. Now she keeps blabbing, but soon it will be words and the world will know what kind of person she is."

Like all babies who change their moods in a constant and intense sequence, Jane would finish speaking, take a breath and burst into tears for reasons known, perhaps, only to herself. Linda automatically responded to wails by sticking a piece of banana in her mouth. Jane switched into a passionate rush of soft, sweet security and banana bliss.

"It's her heroin," Linda said. "It's incredible how important bananas are to her. For example she has only two teeth. Having teeth is a new experience and she's starting to think about what kind of teeth activity to look forward to. When I brush mine in the morning it gets her so excited that she literally becomes ecstatic with pure glee. Sometimes, when she won't stop crying, even with a fix of banana, I just start brushing my teeth and she starts fantasizing again about that day when she too will have teeth to brush. Just like mommy.''

"I guess you're not bored with mommyhood then.''

"Well, I was thinking actually about going back to Holland for a while, 'cause they pay for everything there. The only problem is that the enormous freedom is met by equally enormous passivity. Every once in a while people stop getting high long enough to actually do something quite good, but, you know how Calvinists are, completely without passion unless they are struggling to eat.''

The sun was shining brightly and Jane was so happy eating her banana that Lila began to see hope again in little things, and maybe even in big ones.

"You should check it out Lila. They'll love you there. Lila Futuransky, the girl with the passionately unpretentious aesthetic. But, can you handle a label like that? Can you be the last moral celebrity?''

"Well, check this out Linda, Isabel Schwartz just told me that we've been invited to Nebraska to do The Worst Performance Festival there. They want us to be the imported comic, brunette intellectuals. You know, the conscience of the world routine. We said absolutely not.''

Jane was busy reaching for things that were farther away than she could stretch. She held things too close to her eyes to actually see more than the color. Then Linda stood her up, leaning on a piece of bench, and Jane rejoiced, wide-eyed at the new experience of standing up, until, after a series of revelations about this perspective, she came to realize that she was standing alone. There was trouble on Jane's face, serious trouble, then distress, and finally a look of profound sadness until mommy picked her up again.

"All my life I've fought against dependence of this kind,'' Linda said, giving over the last piece of banana. "But I need to remember that this one is natural, not neurotic. Here Jane," she said, peeling another banana, "have some smack."

FORTY

The third of July found Lila madly back at the typewriter, sweat soaking through her Lily Tomlin t-shirt. The radio was only playing songs with the word *America* in the title. *We're An American Band, America, Living in the USA* and Bruce Springsteen screaming that he was *Born in the USA*, followed by the Statler Brothers singing *My Baby Is American Made*. Lila knew that rock and roll was out of fashion but she loved that fucked up music and promised herself to keep working until they played Bowie's *Young Americans*. She would have done it too, except that Roberta appeared suddenly, sweating and smoking in Lila's living room.

"I've been in this city for two years and now that Muriel's gone I realize I don't know anybody. So, Lila Futuransky, when I wanted to talk, I came to talk to you. I got a postcard from Muriel. She's gotten a job teaching on some hippie farm in the south of France. Her course is called *Improvisational Balance*. I don't know if she's ever coming home."

Lila had the sudden thought that Roberta was a shorter version of herself. If she was writing a play, Roberta would have the lead. If she left town, Roberta would get her apartment.

"It's the clothes. I've been getting constant hassles lately because of my green threads. It's worse without Muriel around because, usually, guys are so busy bothering her, they never come near me. Last night I walked into my lobby, got out my key and the next thing I knew a man was standing next to me, touching me, talking to me, telling me how green turned him on and he wanted to fuck me. I found myself in the ludicrous position of having to struggle to fight him off, just because he had decided on impulse to give me grief. I was screaming at the top of my lungs and eventually somebody came along, but they just stood there and looked. *This is serious* I yelled, *This is serious*. But they kept watching until he got bored and walked away. Just like that. I'm going to kill a man someday."

"That's the second time I've heard that this week," Lila said, rolling Roberta an emergency joint and offering her a shower. She cooked her some noodles with olives and poured a nice cold beer.

"I'm gonna kill a man someday," Roberta said again.

Then they went on to discuss other things because there is always more to a person than what somebody else does to them. They bullshitted and sang doo-wop versions of *The Last Train to Clarksville*. When they were both high-spirited, Lila decided to show off her collection of lesbian trash paperbacks from the fifties and sixties. That was always good for forgetting about troubles.

"You see Roberta," she pointed out, "some are stamped *Adult Reading* and were only available in porn shops or sleazy stores. It was one of the only ways lesbians could read about themselves. First the author would use a man's name, unless really sleazy, then a man would use a woman's name. Sometimes they'd add MD after it for good measure. A lot of them were written like medical discussions of case studies."

"What do you mean?" Roberta asked, opening another beer.

"Like, it would say *I recall my first lesbian client Anna Q. She came into my office to confess to me about a sexual encounter with a nun who passionately tore off her clothes, sucked her tits, ate her through three orgasms, ravaged her neck and left her blissfully dreaming of more.* They describe all this in the most graphic detail of course."

Lila was getting into it so she opened another beer for herself, while Roberta had a second helping of noodles. Lila felt like her older but wiser self.

"Then the patient says how guilty she feels, which reminds the doctor of another case that takes about ten more pages of lurid description."

"Wow," said Roberta, who was obviously feeling better. "These books sound a whole lot sexier than those morality tales we've been fed lately. Let's put the dirt back into dyke drama."

Lila was smiling from ear to ear, pretending she was the underground sex goddess of Lesbiana. Roberta opened another beer.

FORTY-ONE

On the night before the Fourth, the kids and old men and families hung out in the parks and on the stoops and rooftops drinking Budweisers, listening to the radio and shooting off firecrackers all night long. At the center of it was Washington Square Park, hot, dark and full of glory in all its blazing American contradictions.

A Black gay comedian told racist anti-gay jokes to crowds of cheering tourists, and made a lot of money. Break dancers gossiped and squabbled, spending more time negotiating than dancing. A country-western band found they would draw an audience only when they sang Grateful Dead tunes. All this urban conversation was punctuated again and again by ash cans, bottle rockets, rapid fire Chinese fire cracker and sparklers for the little ones out with dad. This went on in between the Rastas selling, buying and playing soccer. Kids, newer than New Wave, with frisbees and guitars, sang John Cougar songs for people who didn't know who John Cougar was. Suburban white people looking for nickel bags stood next to suburban white people who had never heard of nickel bags. Straight couples on dates didn't notice Puerto Rican faggots in mid-drift tops having dramatic jealous scenes and fabulous reunions.

Of course the cops had to come disrupt this natural wonder because, whenever all kinds of people come together for nothing more than fun, the police just have to show themselves, traveling in packs of three, each with a stick and a gun. They just had to come and announce that there would be no more singing in the park that night.

On the way home Lila and Emily stopped for plums.

"I'll buy you a plum," Emily said, as each woman picked out her own. Their plums rested on the counter. Lila's was dark, round with a tone of soft, rich purple. Emily's was tighter, not as ripe, in a shiny reddish skin. When Lila bit into her plum, it split and the inside was warm and sweet as she sucked it out of its bitter shell. It was red, it was golden, it filled every corner of her mouth and oozed its sweetness between her teeth. Then, Emily put her arm around Lila's waist as they walked along.

"There's a sweet dish. One for you and one for me," announced a male voice, emanating loudly from a doorway.

"Lila, kiss me," Emily said. And Lila did kiss her, brazenly and terrified, but she couldn't refuse the power of Emily's embrace and will.

"Thank you darlin'," Emily smiled, triumphant, because she had avoided another defeat, overcoming the violence with pure daring love.

They kept walking through the neighborhood. No matter how dark the sky, it was always day from below, with the store and street lights shining off everyone's eyes. And it never stopped. That was something Lila knew for sure, since one night she had tried to spray paint the latest condo which had displaced six families. At 3:30 in the morning she and Sal Paradise had snuck out, with their spray cans under their shirts and waited all night for the street to empty for five minutes so they could do the job. They ended up sitting there until the sun came up and the club crowds turned into the after hours crowds which turned right into the subway-bound morning work crowds. There was never an empty moment.

"Do you think that gay people will ever be safe?" Emily asked.

That kind of question was so often on everyone's mind that after a while they never actually asked it, just assumed it was always there.

"I don't know. We've always been there. You know I read this great story by Isaac Bashevis Singer, you know, the Yiddish writer."

"No, I never heard of him," Emily said.

"Well, he won a Nobel prize, which is its own story, but anyway, he writes these great stories combining spirits and sex and Jewish ways of approaching things. He doesn't clean anything up for presentation, which, somehow, makes me believe it even more. So, in this story called *Two*, he tells about two boys who met in a yeshiva in Poland and how they fell in love. After studying together and praying together, they separated over a minor jealousy, each marrying an arranged bride as an act designed to hurt the other. After the marriages were in place, they realized their need to be together and escaped to a far away shtetl where they lived as man and wife. One wore women's clothes, lit the shabbas candles and presented himself to the community as a woman. The other carried on a husband's religious and social obligations, presenting himself as a happily married man and pious Jew. Together, praying in their home, they acknowledged to God that they were living in violation of his law but that they still loved him and honored him from the depth of their devotion. Eventually, the one who passed as a woman became well loved in the village as a kind and gentle person. He was eventually given the responsibility of operating the mikvah. There, he happily cut the women's nails and hair and listened to their stories of woe and joy. One night, after many years, a new woman came to the mikvah with a special, fascinating aura. He was so entranced that he reached out to touch her and fell into the water, striking his head and then he drowned.

"When the townspeople learned that he was really a man, they turned from individuals, brethren and neighbors into an angry mob. In a fury, they marched to his lover's house, dragged the terrified man into the street and murdered him. Both bodies were dumped in a hole outside of the town, outside of the cemetery."

"Lila," Emily said, as they continued walking. "Maybe I should stop holding your hand on the street. Maybe it would be safer. I mean, we seem to get hassled by some man almost everyday."

Lila looked around. "Absolutely not. We've got to be together in this. We can't let them come between us."

As she was speaking, Lila felt that sooner or later she and Emily, or she alone, or she and someone else, were going to be attacked on the street and she had to be ready to be hurt and not be surprised.

Lila held Emily's hand tighter, noticing how sleazy the street looked. There was Tony, nodding out in a doorway. His clothes were filthy. During the day, bullshitting around, Lila sometimes forgot that he was really a junkie and sooner or later he would die. There he was, sitting in the garbage and piss, oblivious. He was drooling all over his pants.

They turned the corner past some more buildings in the process of being renovated into condos. The old Orchidia, the world's only Ukranian-Italian restuarant, was all boarded up. The landlord had increased the rent five hundred percent and thrown the owner out on her ass after thirty-two years. There was a rumor that Chirping Chicken was getting ready to open a store on that very spot, or maybe a Steve's Ice Cream so that all the uptown people coming down in cabs would have a place to get over-priced chain ice cream.

Lila and Emily passed a new up-scale bar filled with made-up women and greying men and almost didn't notice the four white kids standing in a line blocking their way. When Lila sensed the barrier, she looked up, almost walking right into two skinheads and their girlfriends. Their leather jackets said *HARD CORE.*

They weren't Hell's Angels types, or even just local toughs. They were rich kids who got turned on by not giving a shit. Vio-

lence to them was a game, not a way of life. The largest, baldest
skinhead was holding out a wooden board, like a weapon, holding it at his crotch and stroking it as if he was jerking off his four
foot wooden prick.

"Just fuck me," he said drunkenly, "just fuck me."

The two women stood still. Neither Emily or Lila could think
of what to do. They didn't know how to talk these kids out of
hurting them for the hell of it. Lila and Emily held each other's
hands as tightly as they could and waited, expecting the wood
to come crashing down on them. Expecting a blur and then a
horrible pain, the splintering of wood. They expected to see
each other crushed and screaming, bloody in the middle of
their own neighborhood, in front of each other.

"Leave those ladies alone," screamed a slurred and pained
voice from across the street. Someone was coming towards
them, walking right into the middle of all that tension.

It was Ray, bloated and sick looking, stubbles of grey growing
out of his shaved head.

"Shut up nigger," said the wooden hard-on, but the moment
had passed. Ray had diffused the violence by crossing the
street. "Come on," the kid said to his friends, and they went
looking for something else to do that night.

"They shouldn't talk like that to nobody," said Ray.

He was wearing a shirt from the men's shelter and Lila
flashed on all the times, in rain and snow, that she had stopped
to talk to Ray, busy selling on the corner and never invited him
up, not even for Thanksgiving. Because she knew that ultimately junkies rip you off. They move in and then they rip you
off. A junkie's mind revolves around getting enough money for
junk, and Ray the junkie had saved her and she had no way of
thanking him, because all that his life boiled down to was cocaine.

"Ray, you saved us, just by saying something. So many people won't even say something."

"I'm sick Lila. You know what I'm telling you. I'm all fucked
up."

And then he looked her right in the eyes and they understood each other perfectly. He was going to ask her for money and he knew that she would turn him down, because in her mind that was not a favor and meant nothing.

"I'll be alright tomorrow," he said. "People are fucking blind. They look at each other and only see color or whatever your thing is. You girls be careful now."

And he was gone into the darkness.

"Is he going to be alright?" Emily asked, wondering the same thing about herself.

"Eventually he's going to die. But we have to watch him get a lot worse before that happens."

Right then, another figure stepped out of the shadow, from nowhere, from the background glare of the steetlights, from the pink neon bagel at The B&H Dairy. It was an old, stooped-over woman, in an old wig and cheap, gaudy earrings. She wore a robin's egg blue polyester dress and shoes that could have been sold for fifty bucks in an antique clothing store. She was garish in her make-up, but approached Lila and Emily as if she had always known them. She spoke in the thickest Southern accent, coming so close to their faces they could smell the cheap toilet water.

"Good evening ladies," she said, in slow measured tones, like a television parody of southern gentility. "Ayh only need a dollah to get home. Would you young ladies be so kahnd as to help me with a dollah? Ayh am eighty-five years old this year."

"It's Blanche," Emily said, reaching into her purse and then handing over the whole purse. The woman grabbed the money and walked away before anyone could change their mind, but after a safe distance, she turned and smiled again.

"Ayh thank you kindly."

"Do tell," Emily said, staring after the disappearing figure. "Blanche, Blanche Dubois. So, you made it to the East Village, Blanche. Take your dollah. Now you can go home to the BMT or Grand Central Station or wherever you live. The Tarantula Arms, was it? Go home to your park bench Blanche. Go home."

Lila and Emily walked quietly for a minute. Then Emily turned to Lila.

"As long as someone knows where you are and worries when you're not home, you can't get too lost. Otherwise we all end up displaced."

As they were making love that night Lila thought that the more she had sex with Emily the more turned on to her she became, building an erotic fascination with every aspect of Emily's body and sensibility. As Emily rubbed her velvet breasts against Lila's breasts, pressed her wet cunt right into Lila's wet cunt, pushed her fingers into Lila's asshole, holding her every way, inside and out, Lila discovered that Emily's nipples smelled of sweat cream, and her neck a mixture of cocoa butter and tea rose, that their bodies fit together perfectly, that Emily's caresses carried her beyond knowing where she was being touched. When Emily sat up against the wall to hold Lila and make love to her, as though her hand was Lila's hand, helping Emily to curl up into her softness, Lila felt her cunt rise up into Emily's fingers, leading her body over her head, clit first, losing all sense of boundary. When Emily made love to her, Lila screamed so loud that hearing that sound come from her own throat was as liberating as any orgasm. It was knowing that she had sought this woman out, night after night, because she wanted Emily's hands between her legs, because she wanted Emily's fingers inside her, because Lila loved Emily's wrinkles, her unspeakably beautiful breasts, her grey hairs, the thrilling shape of her thighs, because Lila wanted Emily's hands tracing her stretch marks. It was knowing she had sought her out and now Emily was in her.

FORTY-TWO

The next morning Lila climbed up on her roof and sat there in the hot sun, looking out over the city. She felt very quiet. Her city was the most beautiful woman she had ever known, and yet, it was changing so quickly. More quickly than Lila was changing or perhaps in different directions.

Lila Futuransky had become responsible for another person. That meant making compromises, giving up things. In return she supposed she'd be a better person. She wouldn't be lonely anymore or horny or friendless. She would be a loved and understood person in this world, which is no small thing, and she would have a great companion. Everyone has to grow up sometime. Sooner or later she'd be almost thirty. Most women her age had families, now she would have one too.

A tear formed in Lila's gut. *I don't know who I am right now,* she thought. *I want to go back to the old way.*

She heard the rooftop door creak open and turned to see Isabel Schwartz step out in her lavender cut-offs.

"Isabel, what are you doing here? Aren't you supposed to be at Burger Heaven?"

"I quit," she said, with an expression of pure happiness. "I spent all night reading *On The Road* and then I went out this morning and saw everyone in the city get ready for another day or get pushed into another day that they'll never be ready for and, do you know what I realized Lila? Do you know what hit me?"

Lila sat quietly, never moving, while Isabel danced around the roof, pointing to the skyscrapers and tenements, using the bridges as her blackboard.

"Lila, think about every kind of person that you can possibly imagine. Then, take the ones who have enough guts to get out of wherever they are because they're driven by a higher fantasy of what is possible, or because the people around them throw them out. Then these individuals come here to a giant cacophony of sound and light and activity and they find out that what they imagined doesn't exist at all. But, there is something even more frightening and holy which is the spectacle of all these people having this realization *together*. Lila, you can't stop walking the streets and trying to get under the city's skin because, if you settle in your own little hole, she'll change so fast that by the time you wake up, she won't be yours anymore. Do you see Lila? Do you see? Lila? Lila? What's wrong?"

Lila stared at her own feet, she was too ashamed to show her face.

"Someone is asking me to do something that will never be right. And I'm going to do it because I love Emily, even though I don't know what that means. And all along I'll know that it will be an endless series of proofs that will never be enough. And my only excuse is that everyone has to do this sometime in their life."

"Don't do it buddy," Isabel was prancing, she was singing like Sal's saxophone, touching the whole neighborhood.

But Lila was sobbing so hard, she was swimming through her tears.